FINAL IMPACT

JACK HUNT

DIRECT RESPONSE PUBLISHING

Published by Direct Response Publishing

ISBN-13: 978-1978109056
ISBN-10: 1978109059

Also By Jack Hunt

The Renegades

The Renegades 2: Aftermath

The Renegades 3: Fortress

The Renegades 4: Colony

The Renegades 5: United

Mavericks: Hunters Moon

Killing Time

State of Panic

State of Shock

State of Decay

Defiant

Phobia

Anxiety

Strain

War Buds: Under Attack

War Buds: On Alert

War Buds: Overcome

Blackout

Dedication

For my family.

Chapter 1

Their world ended long before the catastrophic event. Felicity Meyers was the first to awake to confinement, darkness and the stench of death. Her mouth was dry, and there was a high-pitched ringing in her ears. Her mind tried to grapple with the chaos. A heavy mass pressed down, pinning and smothering her. A dark shape lurked beyond her eyes. It took a few seconds to realize, and then she recognized it as a woman.

The mangled face stared back — eyes open, void of life. She attempted to scream — but could only croak.

As she tried again, a sharp pain jarred the rest of her senses awake. Jagged metal stabbed her arm like the tip of a blade.

She groaned and twisted beneath the unknown weight. Felicity touched the cut on her arm, and that's when she noticed the blood was dry. *How long have I been in here?* Memories flooded in like scenes from a drawn-out nightmare. The past replayed in snippets, only the essentials, only the things the mind could access while under duress.

Arriving at a pyramid-shaped hotel in Vegas.

An argument with a man.

Dazzling casino lights.

Entering an incline elevator.

A tremor then… screams.

Felicity looked at the contorted face of an older woman, her body curled in a fetal position, and jagged metal protruding through her midsection. It stopped inches away from her face.

Reality set in hard and fast.

She'd been in an accident, was in an inclinator, and she was alive but how? Disoriented, Felicity knew she had to crawl out but which way was up?

Below her, a tangled mess of arms and legs answered that. The less fortunate must have acted as a cushion against an impact? Had it dropped? She figured the bodies had saved her life — and perhaps the angle of the inclinator.

How long had she been unconscious?

Her body twisted until she saw a flicker of light breaking through a prison of arms and legs. Her chest felt like it would collapse from being trapped. Her legs — she couldn't feel them. No, no… was she paralyzed?

Panic rose in her chest as she used every ounce of strength to claw her way towards the light. As she turned from a position that was almost upside down, she felt the blood rush from her head, bringing life back to her numb limbs. That's when she could move her toes. A wave of relief flooded her. Her entire body ached as she continued to push limbs out of the way and fight to reach the surface. Slowly she clawed out of the human coffin and shifted herself against the side. Finally, she could take in her cramped surroundings. The inclinator elevator was a six-by-eight-foot space, and seven other bodies hid the floor. The surrounding mirrors were shattered and chunks of shiny gold metal were twisted and crushed beneath concrete.

Fluorescent pot lights flickered above her, threatening to stop working at any second.

Cautiously Felicity clambered over to where the buttons were and pressed one labeled emergency but got no response. Frantically, she ran her hand over all of them but nothing worked. The thirtieth floor was the highest floor, and the screen that usually showed what floor they were at wasn't lit up. She smacked it with a clenched hand but nothing happened except the elevator car shifted a little. A shot of fear coursed through her — the thought she might not be on the lowest floor. Inching back, she pressed herself against the side of the steel coffin.

Immediately her mind went into overdrive thinking of how to escape.

Phone.

She fumbled through her pocket until she felt it.

Instant relief. She was saved. She'd phone down to the front desk, and they'd have a crew up and she'd be out of there in no time. Her phone turned on but the power was on red, it was about to shut off. Damn, how long had she been in there?

She tapped in the digits for the hotel but it didn't ring.

C'mon! She tried again, this time a different number, the one for her apartment.

Again, nothing.

You've got to be kidding me. She clenched her jaw then let out a scream before banging the side with her fist. A jolt, the groan of cables and she shivered, another cold shot of fear. Was the inclinator suspended; hanging on by a thread?

Looking back at the phone she saw the last voicemail, she tapped it and it played back.

"Hey hon, I need to speak to you. It's important. Call me."

There was another one dated a day later.

"Felicity. Did you get my message? I need to speak to you, this is urgent."

One more.

"Please, come home. Please."

Her heart sank. She couldn't believe she was in this mess. Her life couldn't get any worse. If there was a rock bottom, she had hit it a long time ago.

Knowing she might have to use the light of the phone to see her way out of the hellhole, she powered it down. Gazing at those trapped inside she wondered how many of them were dead. No one was moving. It was clear how some of them had died, a large chunk of the elevator car had twisted back, and several beams of steel had punctured through, slicing and impaling.

"Hello? Is anyone alive?"

No response. She focused in on the chests of those who weren't discolored to see if any were breathing. That's when she noticed one of them was. The cabbie, the same guy that had been a thorn in her side from the moment she'd arrived at the hotel.

Then, her eyes drifted to a man who'd been on top of her — well dressed in a dark blue suit, overweight but a good-looking guy in his early thirties with a full head of hair.

Do either of them have a phone on them?

She leaned forward and gave the businessman a shake to see if he would wake but he didn't budge. Felicity rooted through his suit jacket pocket but it was empty. Next, she tried the cabbie. She had her hand stuffed inside his rear jean pocket when he groaned.

Felicity snapped her hand back and shuffled away.

He was alive.

Chapter 2

"Don't you dare tell me I didn't give you enough warning!" Dr. Charlie Meyer bellowed. "I sent the details over a year ago. There should have been an announcement. Why have you waited until now to tell me?"

"It was being handled."

"Then I must have been asleep when the president addressed the nation."

"Do you really think they would send the world into a state of panic unless they were absolutely certain it would hit?"

"I don't know how much clearer I could have made it."

Dr. Charlie Meyer was in his early fifties; short, a full head of hair, a good amount of salt and pepper near the temples. His work as a teacher and astronomer with the FAU Astronomical Observatory at Florida Atlantic

University had garnered him numerous awards over the years, along with recognition from his peers after creating the Space Agency's Global Spaceguard program which connected professional and amateur telescopes looking for smaller NEOs (Near Earth Objects). The nationwide network had been the first to spot DA14, an asteroid that skimmed closer to the planet than any other known asteroid back in February 2013. It was estimated that had it hit the earth it would have released the energy equivalent of 24 million tons of TNT and wiped out 750 square miles.

"I'm sorry, Charlie, I don't know what to tell you."

He slammed his fist against the table. "Tell me the truth!"

"The data was off, Charlie. Radar astrometry has improved, but it doesn't tell us everything. Steps were taken by NASA, now if everything had gone to plan, we assumed it would skim pass the earth based on the trajectory and gravitational pull."

Charlie stared back at him in disbelief. He couldn't

even comprehend what he was hearing. "Gone to plan?"

"Look, we did everything we could. You said it yourself. There were only two options: destruction or deflection — it was too damn big to destroy completely, you and I know that. Even if they nuked it and broke it apart completely, it would have merely scattered the debris turning the damn cannonball into buckshot."

"I told them that."

"And so did I. But they decided to try and destroy it."

"When?" Charlie yelled. "Before they made preparations to save their own asses?"

William sighed and ran a hand over his forehead. "The continuity of government has to happen."

"And what of the continuity of billions of lives?"

"Arrangements have been made."

"I bet they have. And who decides who lives or dies?"

William Baxley was a longtime friend of Charlie's. He was also the head of NASA's NEO program office, a division of NASA that prided itself on being able to predict the path of an asteroid. "Predict" being the keyword, as this time around they'd screwed up.

"You know the answer to that."

"Can you live with that, William?"

He shook his head and walked around the office desk in the underground base of Cape Canaveral. "This is out of my hands, Charlie. There is nothing that can be done."

"Of course there is."

"You still don't get it. After the detonation, it began to reform. So they tried to deflect it by blowing the nuke up next to the asteroid, hoping that it would shove the rock away from earth without creating smaller meteorites. It didn't work. The breakage, the smaller meteorites, that's what has caused the quakes. It's just the beginning. It's still coming. We got it wrong."

Charlie was dumbfounded. He couldn't believe what he was hearing. "Got it wrong?"

"Damn it, Charlie, we have never dealt with anything of this magnitude. All our assessments of previous asteroids have been spot on. And those that didn't pass by the earth, burned up in the atmosphere. Hell, they were too small to be of any concern. But this? What the hell did you expect?"

"Transparency. I expected them to alert the country. People have a right to know."

"And create panic? We are talking about an asteroid that could wipe out over seventy percent of civilization. Like I said, the mission failed, there is nothing we can do now. Mistakes happen."

"Mistakes?"

Charlie ran a hand over his head and paced back and forth in his office.

"They are calling it DA29."

"I don't care what they are calling it. There is still time. Get the president on the line."

"Even if he could make an announcement, no one will hear it. It's too late. The power grid is down in many parts of the country, Charlie. Why do you think I had you travel here ahead of time?"

"How long?"

"What?"

“How long have you known?”

“It doesn’t matter.”

“Like hell it does.”

“Charlie, listen, there is still time for us. There is enough room on those airships for over one hundred thousand people. I’ve already got your name on that list. The military is working with state and city law enforcement to evacuate the pre-selected group. That’s the only way we will survive this. We’ve got to get off this planet.”

“Off? What about my daughter?”

“I’m sorry.”

Chapter 3

"Son of a bitch!" Zeke Blackstone said rolling to one side, and spitting dust. He was on the thirtieth floor, at least he could remember that. His back was in agony. A large mirror, along with drywall had collapsed on top of him. What an end to a hellish evening. He faded in and out of consciousness, the past replayed in his mind as if searching for some sense amid the chaos.

That day had started like any other.

Two shows a day, one in the morning, one in the evening.

He'd been performing his live magic show, *Real or Magic,* at the Luxor for years — ten to be exact. It was part of a long-term contract he'd secured after having huge success on TV. Until that point, everything had been going well. Life was good by any measure. He had the penthouse suite on the top floor of the Luxor, he rarely slept alone, he owned four sports cars and had recently purchased a mountaintop mansion in his own spot of paradise overlooking the Vegas strip.

But that all changed when his contract came up for renewal.

Damn you, Jerry!

He felt himself getting angry again at the betrayal.

His manager, Jerry Sanchez, had pulled him into his office, twenty minutes before he was about to go on stage, to drop the bombshell. He sat behind his desk, wearing a black suit and a pair of oversized gold specs balancing on his bulbous nose. He was one heartbeat away from a heart attack.

"What do you mean they're not going to renew the contract?"

"That's what they said," Jerry replied with a mouth full of BLT.

"They are committing entertainment suicide. Get him on the phone, I want to speak to him myself."

"I can't do that, Zeke."

Zeke got up and stormed towards the door.

"He's not here, Zeke."

With a hand on the knob, he cast a glance back. "Come on, Jerry, this is bullshit. Seriously. They are replacing me with a nineteen-year-old kid?"

Jerry shrugged and wiped the corner of his mouth with a napkin. "He's hot. The next big thing."

"The next big thing? I'm the big thing. I'm the one who sells tickets, who fills seats and ensures that the hotel rooms in this shithole are filled. You think a kid will outsell me?"

Jerry sighed. "He already has. Tickets are sold for the next year. You haven't been able to do that in what? Seven years. Most days we are lucky to get a hundred people a day between the two shows. The fact is no one wants to see you anymore, Zeke. You haven't produced a new magic trick in six years."

"That's because that masked asshole on TV gave away most of my secrets."

"Still. The kid is doing stuff no one has seen. Hell, not even Blaine, Teller or Copperfield is doing the stuff that this kid does. He's on a different level. He's young, full of life,

good looking and..." He took another bite of his sandwich and thumbed through his smartphone.

Zeke eyeballed him then turned and caught a glance of himself in the mirror. He was in his early forties and dressed like a goth from the '90s — long black hair tangled over one half of his face, tight leather pinched at his crotch, a flamboyant white shirt was wide open and his chest was sporting more gold jewelry than a pimp. Okay, he hadn't updated his look in a while but they could have at least given him a heads-up, some kind of warning. Hell, even low-paying jobs had the courtesy to tell their employees when they weren't performing. But not these assholes, no! They had just bitch slapped him to the curb.

Zeke jabbed his finger in the air trying to get control of the situation.

"They can't do this, Jerry."

Jerry picked up paperwork in front of him and tossed it down. "It's in the contract. It expired two days ago. They can do whatever the hell they like."

"But I should have got notice."

He leaned forward and yelled. "You did. I sent you an email, a letter in the mail, and I told you on four occasions over the past year that this was coming down the line and if you didn't do something drastic, they would get someone else."

He shook his head. "I don't recall that."

"Of course you don't. How could you? You spend most of your days as high as a kite, and drunk."

"Bullshit."

Jerry leaned back in his leather seat looking like a poor man's Elvis. "Do you want me to pull up TMZ, or some of the other news sites? Hell, we had to shut down production for ten weeks after that screw-up you pulled a few months back."

"It was a head rush. I was upside down in a straitjacket."

"Oh, I bet it was. Do you honestly think I'm that dumb?"

"I was fine."

"You were high and drunk. You puked all over three audience members."

"That was nerves."

He shook his head and picked up the contract. "Whatever, Zeke. It's over. Done. Look, you have more than enough money in the bank to retire."

Zeke slumped down in a chair and looked across at him.

"Actually…"

His eyes widened. "Oh, you have got to be yanking my chain. Have you blown through it all?"

Zeke stared off at a photo on the shelf of him and Jerry holding multiple awards. The good ol' days. It all seemed so distant now. "It was a few bad investments. Then I had back tax to pay. Hell, I've even had to put the mansion back on the market. I can't afford to keep it."

"You didn't tell me that?"

"I thought my team would fix it. I got a text tonight telling me it looks like I will have to foreclose."

"But all the cars?"

"Bad accountants."

Jerry chuckled and ran a hand over his face. "Well shit on me and call me a sundae! Welcome to the real world."

There was a long pause as Jerry continued to tuck into his food — nothing but the slapping of lips, and him slurping at a milkshake.

"Come on, Jerry. There must be something you can do. I have given my heart and soul, day and night to this damn company for the past ten years. I have bled for you and this hotel. You owe me."

"I owe you?" He burst out laughing and reached into his drawer and pulled out a bottle of bourbon. He poured himself a glass. "Are you really going to play that card? Don't even get me started on what you owe me."

Zeke got up and shook his head realizing he wouldn't get anywhere with him. Jerry didn't give a damn! "Well, thanks for nothing. I'll move my gear out of the room at the end of the month."

"Actually, you must vacate tonight. The kid gets the room."

Zeke spun around. "Hell no."

"Sorry, it's part of his contract."

"And what about me?"

"Head to the mansion."

"And the show?"

"He's going on tonight." He got this big grin on his face, the kind of look he had ten years ago when Zeke walked into his office. Dollar signs in his eyes. He was a greedy bastard and all he cared about was lining his pockets. There was no loyalty. Oh, he'd said they'd take care of him and make sure that all his needs were met, but that's when he was pulling in the crowds. Zeke stared back at him in disbelief.

"We've already made arrangements and boxed your clothes and a few personal items."

"A few?"

"Everything inside that room is the property of the Luxor. It was on loan, Zeke."

Zeke snapped back into the present. He coughed and gazed down the dust-filled corridor that resembled a house of cards waiting to collapse. The carpeted floor was now at a slant. Chunks of the floor were torn up leaving gaping holes, and the wall on the far side had caved in. He groaned as he attempted to get up. His hand dug into a chandelier that was scattered all over the ground. Small pot lights flickered, the backup generator kicking in. There had only been one time in the past ten years it had to be used and by the looks of it, the generator wasn't going to last either.

He wiped drool from his chin with the back of his hand and squinted into the distance. What the —? Just beyond a pile of rubble was a mound. That's when he saw him.

That little bastard who'd tried to steal some of his personal belongings.

Another flash of memory.

Zeke went in and out of the penthouse suite under the watchful eye of security to retrieve his belongings. He picked up a few items and was told they weren't included. He carried out some of the boxes and placed them in the corridor, laying them down on a silver luggage cart. They weren't even going to give him a hand to get it out. He couldn't believe it. Ten years of blood, sweat, and tears and this was how they treated him.

"It's not personal, just business," Jerry had said.

What a crock of crap.

He'd only stepped back inside for a minute to grab up the next box when he saw the figure dart past the door holding one box.

"Hey!" Zeke called out.

He didn't wait for the two security guards to take action. He bolted out the door and caught sight of a small guy, early twenties, wearing a beanie hat and jean jacket, hurrying towards the inclinator doors. He was hoping to squeeze in before the doors shut but they closed before he got there.

"Oh buddy, you have picked the wrong night to piss me off," Zeke said marching towards him. The thief had nowhere to go. The stairwell was already behind Zeke and he was blocking off the only means of escape by holding out his arms like a sumo wrestler. He got within four feet of him when he suddenly launched the box at Zeke, knocking him back, then plowed into him with his shoulder. Zeke toppled and scrambled after him as the two security guards farther

down the hall did absolutely nothing. "Stop him!" He hadn't made it a few feet when the building shook violently.

It was so sudden, fast and uncontrollable that neither of them had time to brace.

Walls shook, the floor collapsed, then everything went black.

Eventually, Zeke crawled his way through the wreckage. Several sparks erupted, threatening to start a fire. He cast a glance at his watch but the second hand wasn't turning. He tapped it a few times then gave up. As he staggered to get up, he winced as he touched his neck. Zeke dropped to a knee, exhausted and feeling dehydrated. That's when he saw his reflection in one of the many shards of mirror scattered across the ground. His head was sporting a gnarly cut, and the blood had dried. He took two pieces of mirror and tried to look behind his neck by holding one up in front, and one behind. Again, more cuts.

"Security," he muttered, then said it again even louder.

No response.

He looked towards what would have been his room but he couldn't see a damn thing. It was like being inside a fun house, with floors that were buckled and twisted. Large steel beams had crossed over making it virtually impossible to squeeze his way through. He was stuck — him and that bastard thief — with only two ways out: down the inclinator shaft or over a balcony.

Zeke stumbled over to his body. *Please be alive.*

Even though he had wanted to murder him earlier, the thought of being trapped alone in the darkness was too much to bear. He dropped down beside the guy and gave him a shake.

"Hey kid, wake up."

His leg had a serious gash on it, and half of his face was covered in blood. Shaking him did nothing. He peered around at the other doors, all of them were locked, smashed to pieces or blocked by broken drywall. He sat there for a while chewing over his options before getting up and heading over to the inclinator. The doors were buckled. He jammed his bony fingers into the small gap and tried to pry it open. It groaned, and he felt the floor shift a little.

Oh shit.

He remembered hearing accounts on the news from those who'd survived the destruction of the twin towers in New York. One minute they thought they were safe and the next they were falling as the floor gave out. Being crushed wasn't his worst fear, but it was up there in his top five worst ways to die. He envisioned having concrete shear off his legs and bleeding to death. The thought of never seeing his kids. *My kids.* He hadn't thought about them in some time. He snorted. Wasn't that just the way shit happened? It had taken a near-death experience to get him to think about them. Zeke slumped down with his back against the wall.

What an idiot he'd been.

He'd worked so hard to build a career, to get fame and fortune and now none of it mattered. The irony was just fitting. He would die alone, trapped inside the place that had kept him from those that really mattered.

A cough.

Zeke lifted his head.

Then a groan.

Homing in on the noise, Zeke felt a sudden surge of hope. He was alive. That little shit was alive. He scrambled to his feet, hurrying over to help.

Chapter 4

"You trying to rob me?" the cabbie said turning over. As he shifted, the inclinator moved ever so slightly. She put out her hand. At first she said nothing. Felicity was still trying to take stock of her surroundings and the fact they were trapped inside a metal coffin, a coffin that didn't feel secure.

"Don't move."

"Why? You got a gun on you?"

Right then his eyes swept over the floor. "Holy shit!" Fear gripped him and he scrambled away. Instantly the inclinator moved letting out a loud metal clanging noise. The cabbie froze. His eyes reflected the same fear she was feeling.

"I told you. Don't move."

"Are they all dead?" he asked.

She shrugged. "I think so, at least those are, but him," she pointed to the businessman. "He's breathing but hasn't woken up yet."

"How long was I unconscious?"

"Your guess is as good as mine."

"Well, how long have you been awake then?"

"Five, maybe ten minutes. I wasn't trying to rob you, I was checking to see if you had a phone. Mine's nearly dead and…"

The lights flickered above them casting shadows on their faces.

"We need to get out of here."

"No shit."

He turned towards the buttons.

"Already tried them. Don't bother. Looks as if the power is out."

"But the lights."

"Backup generator, I figure. Though it sounds as if it's on its last legs. The lights have gone out several times. Each time it's getting longer before power kicks back in."

"Well, we can't just stay in here."

He yelled at the top of his voice for help.

"It's no use. I've already tried that."

He ignored her and continued until he quit. Besides the occasional groan of the inclinator, there was no sound, which meant no rescue workers. She assumed if it had been a malfunction with the inclinator or a small quake, rescue crews would have been on the scene pretty fast. The Luxor was no fleabag motel. It was one of the top hotels in Vegas. As she sat there, she couldn't hear men shouting, or crews working away.

It was silent.

No one was coming.

"What's your name?" she asked.

"Aamir Kapoor. You?"

"Felicity Meyer."

He nodded and stared down at the phone he'd pulled out. It was dead.

They were alone with their thoughts, and that was never a good thing. She thought back to earlier that night and her arrival at the pyramid-style hotel. Being in the room with the john, and him trying to get her to service him and two other guys for the same price. All three of them were drunk and one of them had struck her across the face and told her to put out or they would force her. Until that point, she hadn't run into any trouble. Working as an escort was meant to pay her way through college. She couldn't believe how low she'd fallen. She thought of her late mother, her dad and the argument with him. She should have listened. But she was young, foolish and lovestruck. She had come to Vegas to get hitched. Her then-boyfriend had aspirations of starting some tour business, and she was going to help. How could she have been so naïve? Seven months after they were married, she caught him in bed with some slut he'd met at a bar. That was the end of that.

The businessman gasped for air, startling both of them.

He shifted and let out a loud cry. Felicity and Aamir stared on, wide-eyed.

"Sir, don't move," Aamir said in a slight Indian accent. "You will kill us all."

The man turned, his left eye was swollen, cut and

bruised like a boxer's. His lip was busted up, and he appeared to be sporting a missing tooth. She recalled him holding up a handkerchief to his face when he'd entered the inclinator. But like most people who rode in elevators, she didn't stare and had just focused on the numbers going up.

He moaned and spat blood. "What the hell happened?"

"Quake, I think," Felicity said.

"Our best guess is that we appear to be suspended in this shaft, so be careful moving. I don't want to die," Aamir said.

"Die?"

"The tiniest movement could end us."

He glanced at him and then at Felicity before raising an eyebrow. His eyes took in the sight of the dead but unlike Aamir and her, he didn't appear shocked by it. He smiled. It was an odd reaction in light of their situation. His words soon shed light on his mindset.

"I knew obesity would eventually pay off."

She wasn't sure if he was referring to himself or the large woman beneath him. Either way, he appeared pleased to be alive. "Is it just us?"

"It seems that way, unless of course the others can come back from the dead," Felicity said in a mocking manner. Both of them looked at her and she was about to look away when the businessman let out a chuckle.

"The name's Ben Ford, and you are?"

"Felicity, and this is Aamir."

He craned his neck from side to side and shifted around causing the inclinator to move again.

Aamir put out both hands. "I said…"

"Ah, don't sweat it, Ahab."

"My name's Aamir."

"Ahab, Aamir, it's all the same." He sniffed hard and dug around in his pocket for a handkerchief to blow his nose. "I know you don't want to move but we will have to if you want to get out of here."

"And how do you suppose we do that?"

He lifted his head. "Through the ceiling. We climb."

Chapter 5

"Get the fuck back, man!" The thief jabbed the knife out in front of him. "I'm not kidding. You come near me and I will cut you."

Zeke put out both hands trying to calm him down. "It's not going to be much use, we are both trapped. Now if you want to survive this, you will need my help, and likewise."

His nervous eyes scanned the immediate area. Debris, rubble, it was a complete mess.

"What happened?"

"Well, you attempted to steal my belongings, I chased you down…"

"Not that part, this. What happened?"

"You don't remember?"

"I…"

Zeke took a step forward. "Just put the knife down."

He chuckled. "And let you overpower me?"

Zeke turned his attention away from him. He clearly had mental issues. "Look, do what the hell you want, just give me a hand over here prying open this inclinator door."

"And why would I do that?"

"Because you and I are stuck on the thirtieth floor and the only way out is down the shaft or over a balcony and at least the shaft has cables."

Zeke moved down the corridor casting a glance over his shoulder a few times just to make sure the lunatic didn't try to rush him. Las Vegas was full of nutjobs. He'd run into plenty of them during his long career. After having a long-running magic show on TV that broke all records for the most-watched show, he had been the talk of the industry. He could do no wrong. In fact, there were moments he had to pinch himself because he thought he was dreaming. But that was the way things worked when you could generate money for the fat cats at the top. As long as you were lining their pockets, it was smooth sailing. The second there was a dip, everyone bailed. People were so fickle. The public had the attention span of a gnat. One moment he was hot, and then the next he was cold. It was like a damn Katy Perry song.

Zeke wrenched on the mangled steel. He turned and could see the guy staring at him. "Well, are you going to help or just stand there?"

He pointed the blade. "You try anything and I will end you, you understand?"

"Yes. Yes. You're tough. I get it. Now would you mind?"

The man frowned and tucked the knife into the back of his dark jeans. He was an odd, scruffy-looking fella. His beanie hat had a hole in it, his T-shirt looked one size too small, or maybe his muscles were bursting at the seams, and his army boots had seen better days. One arm had a sleeve of tribal tattoos going down to his wrist. He could appreciate that. Zeke was covered in his own ink. He got his first one at eighteen and since then had gathered many more.

As the guy gave him a hand prying the door open, he

eyed the knife in his back pocket. He could have grabbed it but he was no fighter. He'd only gone after the guy because he thought security would back him up. Fact was, his attire, appearance and hard-nosed public persona were just one big act. He never had to prove himself as for many years he was surrounded by three bodyguards, so he said what he wanted, did what he wanted and used money to cover his ass. But now things were different. The bodyguards were gone. The money was gone, and the public's fascination had faded.

"By the way, I'm Zeke Blackstone."

"I know who you are," he said in a gruff voice.

"Of course you do, otherwise you wouldn't have been eyeing my possessions."

"Look man, you want to argue or get out of here?"

He shrugged and groaned as the door shifted. Had it not been so twisted, it would have been a hell of a lot easier.

"I'm just saying."

"Well don't. I had my reasons."

He paused and contemplated what he said before he spoke again.

"Drug money?"

The guy stopped pulling. "Oh, so you immediately think because I'm dressed this way, and I grab your stuff, I'm a druggie?"

Zeke shrugged. "Well, are you?"

"Screw you, man," he said before he went back to pulling on his side of the door. Slowly but surely they pried it open. Zeke stepped back as the guy peered down. For a few seconds, the thought passed through his mind of kicking him in the back and sending him down that shaft but it was just that — a thought — the leftover anger from a night that hadn't gone the way it should. There was an order to his life. A way things worked. He wasn't used to problems, challenges or dealing with lowlifes. He had lawyers, bodyguards and managers to take care of all that shit. Now what was he going to do?

"Well, have you got a name?" Zeke asked.

The guy looked him up and down with disgust before

sniffing. "Dexter Reid."

"Dexter? Like the serial killer show?"

His eyes narrowed, and he knew he'd hit a sore point.

Zeke tossed up his hands. "Just joking, man. Trying to make light of a dark situation."

He scowled, then sniffed hard. "You didn't tell me what happened."

"You received one heck of a knock to your noggin." Zeke said as he gazed down into the dark shaft. "I think there was an earthquake."

"Right." Dexter nodded. "So are you going down?"

Zeke pointed at his chest. "Me?"

"Well, you said you wanted to get out of here."

"No, I said I need to get the doors open."

He smirked. "Oh, so you were expecting me to go down? Ah, now I get it. You really are a piece of shit."

"I reject that."

"Reject, accept. I don't care," Dexter said walking away from the door and heading back down the corridor. "Perhaps you should find your own way out, and I'll find mine."

"No, we need to stick together. You know, two heads are better than one."

Dexter looked back. "I would agree, but in this case, I'm thinking I have a little more up top than you."

"I..."

"Reject that? Yeah, I bet you do," Dexter added before he could finish.

Zeke stood there for a few seconds as Dexter ferreted into a pocket and pulled out a pack of smokes. He tapped one out and lit it. Zeke stared on.

"Well? Down you go, unless you have a magic trick that can get us out of this?"

Really? He was pushing his buttons. Zeke gripped the side of the doors and peered down. His stomach flipped. There was nothing he hated worse than heights. Sure, he had done several high-flying acts on wires but he hated it. It was part of the reason he threw up over the audience. Jerry said it was the drink and, to be fair, alcohol was involved but really it was nerves. Just good old fear eating away at him. Zeke looked back at Dexter and sighed before leaning in and hugging the wall of the inclinator shaft. Unlike a normal elevator where the cables would have been in the middle of the shaft, these were closer to the wall. He tried to reach them but they were just out of arm's length. *Damn it!* He didn't want to look like a pussy in front of Dexter, who was watching him with an amused smile on his face.

"Take a run and jump," Dexter said with his foot against the wall and leaning back as if he was trying to get comfy. Zeke clenched his jaw and balled his fists as he walked towards Dexter and then turned back towards the elevator. He stood there for a few seconds running over every sort of scenario that could go wrong.

He could trip and fall to his death.

The cable might snap.

His hands might slip.

Hell, he might not even grasp the cable.

"Well come on, they don't call you the Great Zeke for nothing, do they?" Dexter said with a sly grin on his face.

"How about you shut the hell up?"

"Oooh, touchy."

He could hear him yukking it up.

Zeke narrowed his eyes and prepared to sprint for the opening. He'd done a lot of crazy things in his career as a magician but this was right up there. *You can do this, Zeke, just don't think about it,* he told himself.

Zeke pushed off and ran as fast as he could towards the shaft. Just as he was five feet from the door, he heard a voice echo in the darkness. He stopped and heard laughter behind him.

He put a hand back as he cocked his head. "Shut up. Did you hear that?"

"What, the sound of your fear? Oh, loud and clear," he said before breaking into laughter.

"No, listen."

There was silence. Nothing. Was his mind playing tricks on him? He pressed forward to the edge of the shaft and peered into the darkness.

"Someone is down there," he yelled back to Dexter.

Dexter dropped his cigarette and crunched it below his boot before rushing over.

"Hello!" Zeke yelled, his voice echoing off the walls.

They couldn't see anything because of the way the shaft was at an angle but what came back next was clear.

"Help!"

* * *

Ben dropped back down from the opening above him. "There's someone up there." He smiled and the other two looked relieved.

"Finally. Well, I'm sure the rescue crew will lower someone down and we'll be out of here in the next half an hour. All we have to do is sit and wait."

"Sit and wait? Rescue crew? Just because I heard someone that doesn't mean it's the cavalry. We will have to climb."

"Screw that, I'm not heading up there. No, I say we sit here and wait," Aamir said.

"Look, Ahab."

"My name is not Ahab, stop calling me that."

"Whatever. You want to stay here, be my guest but I'm heading up. There is no telling how long this steel coffin will hold and I for one am not risking another minute. Now give me another lift."

"He's right," Felicity said, trying to get Aamir to see sense.

"No. I'm staying still."

"Best of luck then, but I must warn you, I will be rattling those cables like a mother—"

"I'll go up first, I'm the lightest," Felicity said. "Give me a boost."

Ben dropped and she stood on top of his back and then he rose until her head and arms were outside of the box. She hauled herself up onto the top. It stank like oil and rust; there was also the lingering smell of death. Felicity pulled out her phone and powered it on. It lit up the darkness. For how long? She'd be lucky to get another five minutes out of the darn thing. She placed it between her teeth with the lit screen facing upwards and then tore off a piece of her shirt and tied it around her hands to protect them from getting cut up as she climbed. To say she was scared would have been an understatement. She hated heights but the thought of her life ending in some dark shaft was far worse.

"You okay up there?" Ben shouted up.

"As fine as can be."

"Hello, can you hear us?" a voice bellowed down.

She replied, "Yep. Are you the rescue crew?"

There was a pause before a reply echoed. "No."

Her heart sank. She had high hopes it was the fire brigade, the cops, hell, hotel security would have been good but it wasn't. She looked back down to where Ben and Aamir were, they were arguing about something. She wondered if they had even heard the reply. Ben looked up.

"Is it the rescue crew?"

As much as she didn't want to dampen their spirits, she had to tell the truth. She shook her head.

"Fuck. I knew it," Aamir said.

"Well maybe now you can see why we need to climb.

Now give me a hand. I'm going up."

"I don't think that's a good idea. Two of you on the cables?"

"Look, it's not going to change our situation. Our weight is already adding strain."

"But if you shake those cables, that might be the straw that breaks the camel's back."

"Better the camel than me. I'm out of here, now give me a hand up," Ben said.

"No. I say we wait."

Felicity looked down feeling torn between climbing and trying to help Aamir see sense. He was a stubborn asshole who had followed her into the hotel that night, determined to get paid. The problem was she was low on cash and she figured that he wouldn't mind waiting outside for half an hour while she serviced the john. But he went ballistic and said he would call the cops if she didn't pay. Anyway, he followed her into the hotel. Fortunately, she ended up losing him in the crowd and for a brief while she was free of him but after everything went wrong with the john, she returned to the lobby and ran straight into him.

An argument had ensued and to avoid him dealing with cops, she had convinced him she would get his money. Of course, she wouldn't, she was just going to make another run for it once she got to a different floor and then head down the stairwell but she wanted to do it out of the sight of hotel security. He didn't believe her and so he entered the inclinator at the same time.

"Aamir," Felicity shouted down. "Stop being a stubborn dick and give him a hand up."

"Stubborn?" He shook his fist up at her. "You still owe me a cab fare. And now look. This is all your fault."

"My fault?" she asked.

"If you had paid me, I wouldn't even be in here."

"Oh?"

Ben looked on amused by it all.

"You two know each other?"

"Yes. No. I mean," Felicity bellowed. "Oh for goodness' sakes, just give him a hand."

Aamir stared back at her with a look of death in his eyes before lowering his hands and hoisting Ben up. A feat that wasn't easy to do as he was at least two hundred and thirty pounds.

"Are you coming up?" a voice bellowed down the shaft, echoing off the walls.

"Well we aren't going down," Felicity replied before giving Ben a hand. He then reached down and extended a hand to Aamir. "Come on, give me your hand."

Aamir hesitated for a second before taking a hold and Ben hauled him up.

Felicity peered up into the darkness. Though she had lived in Las Vegas surrounded by mountains and had friends that had invited her to go climbing on weekends, she had never once done it. Not that she didn't like climbing, but falling? Well, that wasn't fun in her eyes. She reached up and shimmied up the cable like a monkey.

Every move was causing the inclinator to shake.

"Careful," Aamir said before mumbling some Indian prayer.

There was no telling if it would drop but if it did, it was game over, and it would cost them their lives.

Chapter 6

It seemed to take forever but eventually they could see the two men peering over the edge. There were no rescue workers with them. No police, no firemen, just more survivors. At least it seemed that way.

"There's no point entering here. The stairwell is blocked," the guy with the long black hair said. "Our best chance is to exit via a door several floors down and hope we can get down through the stairwell, otherwise it's over the edge of a balcony."

She knew what that meant. The idea of going over the edge made her stomach churn. The Luxor was a unique hotel that was 350 feet high. Its unusual pyramid construction and layout was designed in such a way that all the rooms lined the interior walls of the pyramid and each floor had an internal balcony that provided a breathtaking view of the world's largest atrium, 30 stories from bottom to top. It certainly wasn't a hotel for those who had a fear of heights. Once a person stepped out of the inclinator and walked along the corridor, specific spots were exposed to the center of the hotel while other areas were walled off.

Felicity stopped climbing and looked over to Ben who was on the cable beside her.

"We'll try this door."

He reached across to a metal handle and pulled away from the internal shaft and braced himself before extending his hand to her. Both Aamir and her were positioned at a diagonal angle. It was awkward, and one slip could be fatal. She refused to look down.

"Come on," Ben said. "I can't open this door without you."

"I'll do it," Aamir said climbing up and reaching for his hand. He yanked him over and now both were standing on a thin ledge in front of a mangled elevator door. Felicity looked up to the next floor where the other two were.

"You guys coming down?"

"Once you are off the cables. I'm not risking it until then."

Metal groaned as Ben and Aamir gingerly pried open the steel jaws. Once they got clear of the doors, Ben assisted her.

Slowly but surely the two strangers made their way down the shaft and joined them on the next floor. When they came into view, Felicity's brow knit together.

"Aren't you Zeke…?"

"Yes," Zeke said before brushing past her and heading for the stairwell. It was so dark inside that shaft, she couldn't make out who it was until they climbed down.

"I'm Felicity," she said extending her hand to the next handsome-looking stranger.

"Dexter."

After a brief introduction by them all, they set about trying to get out.

Mounds of debris covered the corridor, creating slopes that were hard to get over. Once they made it to the stairwell, they were relieved to find it intact. None of them spoke to one another. They quickly worked their way down the steps hoping to get out and on with their lives. That wasn't to be. They'd got eight floors down before encountering a large slab of concrete blocking the rest of the way.

"Oh, C'mon!" Zeke said kicking it in frustration.

"Yeah, that isn't going to work, Einstein," Dexter said, to which Zeke scowled and slumped down

"Were there any survivors on the floor you were on?" Ben asked.

"If there were, we didn't see or hear them."

"There has to be more people alive. There are over 4,000 rooms in this hotel."

"They are probably either trapped or dead."

Ben climbed back up the stairwell to the next floor to see if there was any other way out.

"It's blocked off. We aren't getting through."

"Shit!" Zeke bellowed slamming his hand against the wall.

"Calm down. It's not going to help to lose your shit,"

Dexter muttered.

He was quick to react. “Don’t tell me what to do.”

“Whatever, man.”

“Were any of the rooms open?” Felicity asked.

“Several.”

“Well as much as I don’t like the idea, I think we should probably gather sheets off the beds, tie them together and go over the balcony.”

“Does that mean you are volunteering?” Zeke asked. “About time.”

Dexter was quick to jump all over that. “Unless you want to stay trapped here, you’re going over too.”

“Like hell I am. You guys can go down, contact rescue crews and they’ll come up and get me.”

“Really? And how do you plan on surviving up here? On cookies and bar nuts?”

“Don’t you worry about me.”

“Oh I won’t,” Dexter replied before following Felicity up the stairs to the next floor. Over the course of the next twenty minutes, they gathered together as many sheets as they could find and tied them together. Some of the rooms they couldn't get in because the structure had taken one hell of a beating. There were steel bars sticking out of the walls, and concrete was blocking the way.

"You think it will hold?" Dexter asked dropping his end.

"Only one way to find out," Felicity said. "Ben, grab a hold of the other end and give it a tug." Felicity wandered down the corridor to the far end of the makeshift rope. The plan was straightforward. They would lower it and climb down several floors, then create another makeshift rope from sheets. That way they didn't have to rely on creating it too long. They just needed enough to get them down a few floors at a time. Felicity tugged hard on one end, and Ben did the same. It wasn't exactly a guarantee that it would work but they had few other options.

"You want to go tell his lord and king we are ready?" Felicity said, mocking the way Zeke was acting like a diva.

"It would be my pleasure." Dexter shuffled away. While they waited, they lowered the tied-off sheets over the balcony and Felicity felt her stomach churn within her. Had it been a regular vertical tower, they would have been able to slip down the sheets and reach the next balcony with their legs but they were dealing with a diagonal angle due to the entire place being in the shape of a pyramid. All of which meant they would have to swing back and forth.

"If I knew this would happen, I would have let the cab fare slide," Aamir said looking green in the face. "I worked for seventeen years as a cabbie in this city and have seen it all; drug addicts, prostitutes, drunks and crazy tourists and I've survived. Now I'm about to fall to my death."

"Ahab, don't you have some belief in a higher power? What about all those gods you worship?"

Aamir scowled at Ben.

"You really shouldn't wind him up."

Just as she said that the door to the stairwell opened and Zeke stumbled out.

"Go on, keep moving."

"I should have kicked you down that shaft when I had the chance," Zeke replied.

Dexter was holding a knife to his back.

"Whoa, what the hell you doing?" Ben piped up.

"Exactly. Thank you," Zeke replied.

Dexter grinned. "He needed a little motivation."

"So you pulled a knife?"

"Look, you asked me to get him. Here he is."

"Finally, others can see how damn crazy you are," Zeke muttered.

"Just put the knife away," Ben said motioning to it with his hand. Dexter didn't hesitate and slid it back into his waistband. The second he did that, Zeke spun around and cracked him on the side of the jaw, knocking him to the floor. He loomed over jabbing his finger in his face.

"You pull a knife on me again, I will jam it up your ass."

"Touchy!"

"Okay. If you two are done having your pissing match, maybe we can get the hell out of here. Now, who's going first?"

They looked at one another and then Ben said, "I will."

"Like hell you will," Aamir spat. "What are you? Two forty, two seventy?"

"Oh Ahab has finally grown balls," Ben said stepping back and waving towards the sheets. "Be my guest."

"I… Well…"

"I'll do it," Felicity said. "I weigh less than all of you."

She climbed up over the balcony edge and tried to not look down.

"Okay, be careful."

She gripped the sheets. Her hands were sweating and she could feel her temperature rise. Felicity took a firm grip on the sheets and gave a sharp tug to make sure it would hold.

Ben leaned over. "We got you."

"Let's hope so," she muttered before stepping off the thin ledge and placing all her weight on those sheets. What did she have to lose? If they remained there, they would starve to death. As she climbed down, only silence permeated the pyramid. By now, those who had escaped would have been far away from this house of cards. Slowly she made her descent, hugging the cotton material.

She stopped for a second and looked up. All four guys were watching her intently. She had to wonder if they were staring down her top or genuinely concerned for her well-being. Perhaps both?

"That's it. You're okay. Keep going."

Once she got down two floors, she swallowed hard. This was it. If anything would go wrong, it was now. The only way she could reach the next floor was to rock back and forth until she built up a steady momentum. Slowly but surely, she began the perilous process. Her heart was thumping in her chest as she reached with the tip of her boot for the balcony. One second she thought she had it, then the next she was swinging back out.

Again she tried, this time having success.

Finally, her foot caught the lip, and she worked her way over until she was safe.

"All right, next one."

Aamir was next. He eased his way down with no problem. Above, an argument ensued when it came to Zeke's turn. Though she couldn't see them, she was sure Dexter had pulled his knife again and was threatening to slit his throat if he didn't go.

One by one they shimmied down until finally, it was Ben's turn. He scaled over the edge and seemed to do okay until it was time to swing over to the ledge.

His foot caught, just as the sheet gave way.

He let out a cry as Dexter and Zeke grabbed a hold of his pants and he slammed into the side. Here he was hanging upside down twenty-one floors above ground. He was cursing at the top of his lungs.

After a fair amount of yelling, barking orders and tense seconds, they pulled him up and over. He collapsed breathing hard and drenched in sweat.

"I am not doing that again."

"I'm afraid you will have to, fat man," Aamir said with a smirk on his face. "It's the only way down." He seemed to be taking delight in his fear.

The fact was, he was right.

After a few minutes rest, they were back at it.

It was a slow process, and there were a few times when they didn't think they would have enough sheets but finally, the ground was reached and then came the next challenge — getting out.

From what they could see, there were no people, no rescue workers and no exits. All around them was dust and darkness. Everything — rooms, slot machines, tables, stores and concrete statues of Anubis — had been turned to rubble. The ground had cracked, massive fissures zigzagged away from them like a spiderweb. How many hundreds of people had fallen into the abyss below? How many were even in the hotel at the time? Just because there were a lot of rooms that didn't mean they were occupied at the time. She figured that many people would have been out on the town, taking in the sights, playing in casinos, watching shows and visiting bars.

Felicity gazed around at the devastation. It was hard to

come to terms with.

Most of the stores were now inside the pool, roofs had caved in on the atrium level and burst pipes had flooded the entire floor with enough water to reach their knees. For as far as the eye could see, there was nothing but a disaster.

Chapter 7

The devastation was on a scale far beyond what she could have imagined. If the inside of the hotel had been torn up, what was it like outside? And where the hell were all the rescue crews? Was anyone out there helping people? How long had they been inside that elevator?

Dexter bent down and picked up a bottle of water, twisted the cap off and chugged it down. Aamir stepped over mounds of debris and tried to stay out of the water.

"Unless you want to get electrocuted, I would stay clear of the water," he muttered.

"That requires power, Ahab. No lights, no power," Ben replied.

"Yeah, well, you say that now. When your ass is toast, you'll wish you had listened."

"No. No, I won't because I would be dead."

"Stupid man," Aamir said ignoring him and hopping from one portion of the collapsed ceiling to another.

While the outside of the Luxor hotel was glass, the inside was marble and concrete. Most of it had cracked and fallen into the center of the pyramid. The atrium itself didn't even look the same anymore. It was hard to tell where it began and where it ended. Whoever had been in the center at the time wouldn't have survived. It would have been like a cave collapsing in.

Thin shafts of daylight filtered through crumpled metal and concrete, teasing them to escape. But it wasn't as simple as that. After an earthquake, everyone was still at risk from the instability of what remained. Felicity knew well that they were standing in a house of cards that could collapse at any minute.

Felicity gripped hold of a table and tried to get her bearings. Right now all that mattered was finding a way out.

Water sloshed beneath their feet from where the place had been flooded.

"Hold on a second," Dexter said, scaling up a large section of concrete.

"Be careful."

"I'm fine," he said as he made it to a small area where light was coming in.

"Holy cow!"

"What is it? What do you see?" Zeke asked.

"You don't want to know."

He scaled back down, his face a pasty white. "Oh my God." He paused for a moment.

"What's going on?" Aamir asked.

"It's a mess outside. Nothing but buildings that have collapsed," he said before slipping down and rejoining the group. As they continued on through what remained, it was getting harder to find any ground that was level. Twisted metal and concrete dominated the floor, creating a maze of walls. Water covered everything, making it slippery and treacherous.

"You see a way out?"

"No, but I see a shitload of bodies." Zeke braced himself against a pillar of concrete and threw up. As Felicity made her way over to see, she diverted her gaze at the horrific sight. There were swollen, severed limbs floating on top of the water.

"Hey!" a voice called out.

All of them looked up and saw a group of hotel guests. There had to be about six of them, eighteen stories up. They were waving.

"Help!"

Slowly but surely, others emerged from some of the rooms. Two couples, a collection of kids and some elderly people. Others had survived but were in the same situation, trapped high up beyond the balconies. After the quake, she figured they stayed in their rooms hoping a rescue crew would come but as no one was here, it meant things were bad. Dexter shouted up that the only way down was to tie together sheets; in the meantime, they would try to see if they could get help.

"Don't leave us!"

"We'll try to get help."

Every few minutes they could hear metal creaking. They didn't need to be involved in construction to know it was the groan of beams weighed down by concrete. Occasionally, a chunk of concrete would drop and cause a massive splash in the water.

"Um guys, take a look at this."

Aamir ran his hand over a sign that was twisted but from what they could discern it was a map of the Luxor. He ran his finger through a fine layer of dust. It showed the main entrance, the north entrance, the east, and the west, which went to the parking garage.

The main entrance was crippled, along with the east, hidden behind a curtain of concrete.

Whatever hope of exiting that way was gone.

The west was blocked too, so that left only the north entrance and the underground shopping mall called Mandalay Place. It was shared by both the Luxor and Mandalay Bay hotels.

Turning to head north, Aamir slipped on one of the concrete slabs and disappeared below the water. "Aamir!" Felicity yelled hurrying over, water splashing up over her knees. It was freezing cold and making her skin numb. It would only get worse the longer they stayed in there. Dexter reached him before she could. He'd slipped beneath two stacked pieces of concrete. One second Dexter was there, the next he had dived head first into the water.

A few tense seconds and then they both emerged, gasping for air.

"Next time don't climb up the concrete with wet shoes on."

Both of them leaned back on the slab and took a few minutes to catch their breath.

One thing was certain, if they didn't get out of there and change into some dry clothes soon, there was a chance they could end up ill. Dexter led the way, using a pole he'd picked up to make sure that the floor below the water was safe before pressing forward.

The closer they got to the north entrance, the more they realized that wasn't going to be an option. Everywhere they turned concrete and metal blocked their way. Glass was shattered, and store walls had collapsed against each other, making it feel even more claustrophobic than it already was. The smell of death lingered in the air.

"How long do you think we were trapped in that elevator?"

"Couldn't have been more than twelve hours. My watch is showing it's the sixth today. Yesterday was the day I was…" He trailed off with a despondent look on his face and trudged on.

As they continued on towards the underground shopping, they were met again with the same sight. Concrete walls and twisted metal blocking their path.

"You have got to be kidding me," Aamir said. "I can't be stuck in here. I have a family. I have a life beyond this place. I was meant to go on vacation. I…" He looked over to Felicity and then it was like a light switch flicked on, he charged toward her, hands out. "I should kill you. This is your fault. If you had just paid me."

Dexter reacted, sticking out his arm. It caught just under the chin, toppling him instantly.

Before he could get up, Dexter was on top of him pushing his head under the water then bringing him back up again.

"You ready to play nice?"

Aamir cursed.

"Blaming people will not get us out of here."

Aamir bellowed in his face. "Let go!"

"Not until you promise you will not act like a child."

He glared at Felicity and then nodded, gritting his teeth. Zeke looked on amused by it all.

"Anyone want to tell me what that's all about?"

"She ducked out on a cab fare and that's why I'm in here," Aamir shot back.

Zeke laughed. "Well isn't that ironic?"

"Shut up, Zeke," Dexter said brushing past him and scaling up a slab of concrete. He peered through some gaps. "Listen, we can get through but it's not going to be easy. It's gonna be real tight."

"You expect me to fit through that?" Ben said. His large frame would cause problems if that was the only way out.

"Like I said, we are running out of options here."

"Why not just enter one of the hotel rooms, smash a window and slide down the outside?"

"Oh sure, and while we're at it, let's grow a pair of fucking wings." He stared back at them before turning and taking off his jacket and tossing it down. "I'll go first, okay? You guys stay here. Sound fair?"

Zeke dropped onto a concrete block, crossed his legs and leaned back. "Knock yourself out. You thieves were always good at squeezing through tight spots."

"What's that supposed to mean?"

"What does he mean, thief?" Ben asked.

"You want me to tell them?"

"Shut up, Zeke," Dexter said before turning and pulling his way through a narrow gap.

"Seriously? What are you on about?"

"Our little ferret of a friend there was trying to steal my belongings just before the quake hit."

"I didn't know they were yours," Dexter hollered back.

"Oh, that makes it so much better."

"Screw you."

"Did he break in?" Ben asked putting up a leg up on a small wall and retying his shoes.

"No, I was taking my stuff out. Moving."

"Moving?"

"Well, evacuating my room. I have a home outside of the Luxor that I bought a year ago but I'm rarely there because of all the hours I've put in at this place."

Felicity stepped forward. "That's right. You've had that long-running magic show. So what's that like? Being on top of the world. Rich and all?"

"When it was good it was fucking fantastic. Today, not so."

"Well, once we get out of this situation, I'm sure you'll be able to pick up the pieces just fine."

"The pieces, right. Yeah, I guess so."

Ben stared into the distance. "Hey look, um. I'm going to find somewhere to take a leak. If he comes back, wait for me."

"You bailing on us, fat man?" Aamir said.

"No Ahab, I'm off to take a whiz."

Aamir snorted. "He's bailing on us," he said before taking a seat. Felicity watched Ben stroll off, climbing over a few pillars and heading in the direction of the casino. Felicity turned back her attention to the stack of boulders and concrete. She was hoping to see Dexter reemerge.

She climbed up and shouted through. "Dexter. Any luck?"

"So far its clear but I don't want to get your hopes up. This might lead nowhere," his voice echoed back. She pulled away and slid back down the broken pillar.

"So what about you?" Zeke said eying her. "What's your story?"

"I was here to see a friend."

"Bullshit, you were here to screw someone but instead you screwed me over for a fare."

"Dear me, Aamir, how much did she owe you? I'll give you the damn money if you just shut up." Zeke reached into his pocket and pulled out a wallet.

"You don't need to do that," Felicity said.

"No, it's not a problem. What? It can't be over twenty bucks."

"Sixty, sixty-two dollars. She made me wait outside."

"I got held up."

"A likely story," he replied.

"Well, I only have forty bucks on me."

"A rich guy like you? Come on."

"I don't carry a lot of cash. That's a one-way ticket to get your throat slit in this town."

Felicity looked off towards the casino. "Hey look, I'm gonna go check on Ben, make sure he's okay."

"Yeah, you do that. Run away like him," Aamir said.

"Aamir. Give the girl a break."

"I did, a two-hour break, and she tried to rip me off."

Felicity shook her head as she crossed through the water over several downed pillars and headed in the direction she last saw Ben. She was wandering for like twenty minutes before she spotted him sitting at a dilapidated bar in the casino area. He was drinking straight from a bottle.

"Hey there," Felicity said coming up behind him. In front of him was a stack of cash, hundred-dollar bills all wrapped up. The second he heard her, he shoved them into his pockets.

"That's a lot of cash you got there."

"It's what these bastards owe me."

"Really?"

She took a seat beside him on one of the stools.

"Can I get a drink?"

He shrugged, reached over and grabbed a glass among those that weren't broken or scattered on the ground. He filled it with two fingers of bourbon and slid it down.

"So were you here on business or pleasure?" Felicity asked.

He chuckled and took a large gulp of his drink before filling it up again.

"Both."

"What do you do for a living?"

"What *did* I do?"

"Yeah, that's what I meant," Felicity said.

"I was a salesman for cash registers. You know, the things that take the money and whatnot. It's a tough sell nowadays with the latest technology. The traditional cash register is heading towards becoming obsolete."

"Technology. Like?"

"Smartphones, tablet computers. Hell, all they need now is the credit or debit card. A quick swipe and the money is in their bank. Cash is on its way out."

"Maybe not now."

Ben nodded before knocking back his drink and pouring another. "True. Perhaps we might see a resurgence in cash register sales though I wouldn't bank on it."

"Depends on what's happened here."

"I'm sure it's just a minor earthquake."

"And if it's not?"

He patted his pockets. "Well, I guess this cash won't be much use."

There was a pause as they continued to drink.

"So what else?"

"What do you mean?"

"I asked if you were here for business or pleasure. You said both."

He pulled out a pack of cigarettes and offered her one but she declined. He took it, placed it between his lips and lit the end. After a long drag on it, he blew out smoke.

"I was playing cards. Trying to win enough money."

"To get out of what you do for a living?"

"Nope. To pay off loan sharks I owe."

"Oh?"

He knocked his drink back. "Yeah, not the best position to be in but hey, things could be worse," he said gazing around and then laughing.

"So that's why you want the money."

"Oh, believe me. If I get out of this, those assholes aren't getting one cent of this. I'm disappearing. Perhaps I'll buy a yacht and go spend my days on some island in the Caribbean."

"And spend your days being chased?"

"Well let's hope they didn't make it. Miracles can happen, right?"

"Right. So why were you heading up in the elevator?"

He breathed in. He tapped his finger against the mahogany bar that was chewed up by fallen debris and covered in a thin layer of dust. "Nothing escapes your eye, does it?" he said before continuing. "I was…"

Before he could finish what he was about to say, Zeke called out.

"Guys, Dexter has made it through. Let's go!"

Chapter 8

It seemed to take forever to squeeze through the mangled mess of rock and metal. It was a game of inches, and a great degree of luck. The air inside was practically nil. Minimal airflow made every inch forward feel like they were climbing a mountain. Felicity was reminded of her ex as she clambered through. In the weeks leading up to their separation, Jarrod had taken her out climbing in the foothills of Red Rock Canyon National Conservation Area. They'd come across several caves and one that had a section called the letterbox due to its shape and the fact climbers had to remove their helmet and backpack if they wanted to squeeze through. It had scared her to death but not as bad as this. This was far worse. She could hear the rock around her shifting, dust drifted into her face and Felicity coughed up a lung.

"How are you doing, Felicity?" Dexter hollered back.

"Just dandy," she said before pressing on, sliding

around a large pillar. Her head and shoulders got through but her hips weren't having any of it. She wiggled and tried to push her foot against more rock, but that only caused more dust to fall.

Eventually, she squeezed through, cursing every step of the way. All of them were, Aamir was the worst. She could hear him muttering to himself in his Indian language and then every few seconds blurting out an F-bomb. She kind of felt bad for the guy. It was true if she had paid him off, he wouldn't have been in this mess. But how the hell was she meant to know that it was going to turn out this way?

"That's it, keep coming," Dexter coaxed her through the final section. "Now you are going to slip but I'll catch you."

He was right. As she dangled out, bent over and hanging down the slope, she felt herself slip and fall headfirst into the knee-deep water. When she emerged from the water Dexter was looking a little sheepish.

"I thought you would catch me?"

“Sorry, I misjudged it and my foot slipped.”

“My fist will slip in a minute,” she said before breaking into a grin.

One by one they emerged from the womb-like enclosure to a spacious area full of stores. The air was thick with dust, it was like walking onto a construction site where they were drywalling. Felicity pulled her top up over her face while she waited for Ben. He was the last one through. As he crawled out and pushed his feet against a section of concrete, there was an almighty crack, then rubble gave way.

“Go, go, go,” Dexter shouted to him, realizing that it would collapse.

She’d never seen Ben move so damn fast. His chubby fingers raked at the rock below him like an army guy in boot camp scrambling below barbed wire and taking in mouthfuls of dirty water. Aamir and Dexter reached and grabbed him by his arms and tugged him out, seconds before the hole closed behind him.

A huge waft of dust billowed out.

Gasping for air, Ben placed his hands on his knees as he remained in the water, before splashing some of it over his face and then touching his pockets. "Shit. Shit!"

"What?" Zeke asked.

"The money. The money, it's gone."

He got down on his knees and swept his hands in an arcing motion, frantically searching the water.

Aamir laughed. "Oh man, you are funny. I'm glad I'm not the only one who's lost money tonight."

"You took money from the casino, didn't you?" Zeke said cluing in.

Ben didn't answer that, he was too busy fretting.

"Give it up, man, it's not going to be of much use to you wet."

Ben let out a loud cry. "Aha!"

He raised up a brick of cash that was soaked. "Here, Felicity, hold this, the other one has got to be here." She took it and looked at him like he was some kind of crack addict searching the floor for his next hit.

He never found that second brick.

After searching for close to half an hour, he concluded it must have dropped out while he was squeezing through the narrow gap. The four of them pressed on and after about ten minutes, and traveling up a slight incline, they finally ended up on dry ground.

"I'm starving. What about you all?"

"I want to get out of these wet clothes."

They stuck to her body like a million tiny leeches. Dexter nodded to a clothing store. Its main window was shattered, and several of the mannequins were crushed below a mound of rubble.

"Well, I always wanted to shop without paying." She smiled and stepped into the clothing store. It was hard to see anything inside. The only light came from her phone, and that was at the point of giving up the ghost.

"We need to find some flashlights."

"I'll go check," Zeke said heading out of the store and disappearing out of view.

She snagged up a few items that looked like they might fit. A pair of jeans, a T-shirt, and a warm hoodie, along with a jacket and underwear. The others did the same. Though the situation wasn't any better, doing something that they had done before seemed to lighten the mood. Felicity snagged up a few pieces of clothing to towel herself dry before heading into the changing room.

Five minutes later she came out feeling like a new woman. Her clothes would get torn and wet again, but at least her entire body wasn't soaked. Staying wet was the quickest way to end up ill, and right now she couldn't afford that.

"Not bad," Ben said. "You clean up well."

She tied back her hair into a ponytail. "You too."

He now looked preppy in his tan khakis, white sneakers, blue and white boating shirt and red jacket.

"Look what I found," Zeke said stumbling in, nearly tripping over. He was holding four flashlights and several packs of batteries. "Well look at all of you."

"You gonna change?" Aamir asked him.

"Into those cheap threads? Hell no, I would rather stay wet."

Aamir shrugged. "Suit yourself."

As they made their way out, Zeke peppered them with questions. "So you didn't tell me where you all come from? Are you here on vacation?"

"I'm based in New York," Ben replied. "No kids. No wife."

"No? How come?"

"Too busy with work. I never got around to it. And you?"

"Three kids, three failed marriages and a girlfriend that just recently left me."

"Sounds like I'm not missing anything," Ben said before chuckling.

"Trust me. You're not." He then looked over to Dexter. "And what about you, my light-fingered friend?"

Dexter tossed him a scowl.

"Ooh, brooding. Actually, don't tell me, let me guess. You have a crib north of Las Vegas that you share with your homeboys, and it's packed with all the highest-end merchandise. Products that you stole of course, but nevertheless, top of the line. Am I getting warmer?"

"Screw you, Zeke. You don't know me."

"Oh, I think I have a good idea."

"Yeah? Oh, that's right, you read minds as part of your magic act." Dexter turned, so he was facing him but walking backward. Felicity was beside him. "So, how about you guess how many fingers I'm holding up?"

Felicity laughed as she could see he was flipping him the bird with both hands.

"You know what, Dexter, who cares where you're from. What about you, Aamir? You got a little honey at home? I figure you as a big family man. Nine kids. Am I right?"

Aamir was kicking small pieces of stone across the ground as he pressed forward. "I am married, with four kids and I've lived here in Las Vegas my whole life." He reached into his pocket, pulled out his wallet, retrieved a photo and handed it off to Zeke.

"Nice. What is that, wife number four? Don't you folks marry several women?"

"No. That's my first and only wife."

"Yeah, some guys can actually perform in bed," Dexter said, holding his hand out and Aamir slapped it.

"Hilarious," Zeke shot back before handing the photo around so everyone could see.

He sniffed hard. "And what about you, princess? You got a man at home to keep you warm at night?"

She eyed him and smiled, shaking her head. "Nope."

"No, you're not married? Or no, you don't have a guy?"

"Both."

"But you had one, right?"

She focused ahead looking into the darkness. "I had one."

"He dumped you for another woman, didn't he?"

"No, he thought he could have his cake and eat it too."

Zeke studied her face. "You found him in bed, didn't you?"

She shook her head and laughed. "Maybe you can read minds."

"Shit, I knew it. Dang, that's what Las Vegas will do for you. So many come here with dreams of making it big and they either succeed or fall flat on their ass and if they do, they will take you down with them."

"Is that what happened to you?" Aamir asked.

"Actually, no, Aamir. I'm one of the few who succeeded for a time."

"So that new kid took your place."

He frowned. "How do you know about that?"

Aamir talked about himself in the third person. "Oh, Aamir sees more than you know. Aamir saw the billboards around town. He saw them taking your mugshot down and replacing it with that new, fresh-faced kid. How old's he? Eighteen, nineteen? A good-looking kid and what, you're in your late fifties now?"

Zeke dropped his chin.

"Aamir," Felicity muttered and shook her head.

"Oh so he can chew into us but we can't give it back to him?" Dexter asked.

Felicity stopped in her tracks, her flashlight beam

washing over the way ahead of them. They all noticed it. It was blocked off. "No. No!" Zeke yelled. He kicked a soda can across the floor and then picked up a large chunk of concrete and tossed it through a window. "Fuck!" His voice echoed loudly.

It also didn't help that bloodied legs and arms of victims, covered in a fine layer of dust, extended out from beneath the rubble.

"What now?" Ben asked.

"I'll tell you what now, we are royally screwed," Zeke said. "I knew we shouldn't have moved from where we were. Eventually, the rescue crew would have shown up and smashed a window and got in and…"

"Oh shut up, Zeke," Dexter muttered. "Unless you have an idea how we will get out, why don't you give those gums a rest? They've been flapping non-stop since I woke up."

Zeke stared for a second and then charged him. "I'm gonna rip your head off."

"Hey, hey!" Ben got between them along with Felicity.

"Fighting will not get us out of this situation. We need to work together. Okay?" When Zeke didn't reply, Ben repeated, "Zeke? Okay?"

"Whatever."

"Look, maybe we should try to find something to eat and drink. I can think a lot better on a full stomach," Ben muttered.

"It looks like its full already," Aamir said.

He pointed at him. "Don't you start!"

As Felicity washed her beam over the ground, she noticed a trail of blood had trickled down from one of the bodies creating a mini stream. She bent down and picked up a wallet, dusted it off and flipped it open.

"Maggie Roberts, age 52." She pulled out a photo of her and some grown-up kids. How many had died down here? The loss of life had to have been in the high hundreds. As she fished through more of the bags and belongings buried beneath dust, she took a moment to wonder what their lives were like. The others rooted through the stores nearby searching for anything to eat.

"Found a seafood restaurant," Ben hollered.

"Yogurt, anyone?" Zeke said coming out of a store with a tub in his hand and a spoon.

Over the course of the next hour, they devoured a few plates full of cold seafood they'd pulled out of a fridge laying on its side. They washed that down with a couple of cans of Guinness from a place called the Ri Ra Irish Pub.

"You know what?" Ben said. "I know this is a fucked-up situation but I am glad we're in it together. It could be worse."

That got a smile out of all of them.

"I'll toast to that," Dexter replied lifting his black can of Guinness.

Zeke turned to Felicity. "So you didn't say if you lived in Las Vegas or elsewhere?"

"I moved here eighteen months ago with my asshat boyfriend. After we got married, we lasted a whopping seven months before I caught him in the sack with some girl he'd been seeing for three more before that."

"What was his excuse?"

She was a little tipsy from the Guinness and with her inhibitions low she just let it out. "Said he had fallen in love and there was nothing he could do about it. Can you believe that? Oh, and her tits were bigger than mine." She placed her can down and cupped her breasts. "Do you think these are too small?" She glanced at them and all four of them shook their heads.

"No, they are perfectly fine, Felicity. Believe me, I have seen my share of breasts in my time," Zeke said.

"Thank you, Zeke, I will take that as a compliment." She raised her can and made a toast. "Here's to shitty boyfriends and ignoring texts."

"Hear, hear, except for the part about boyfriends," Dexter said.

"Ignoring texts?" Aamir asked.

"Oh, my father. Yeah. For the past year, he's been sending me these crazy texts about how I needed to head to Florida, come home because there was some big thing about to happen and... Well, it's just my father. He never wanted me to marry Jarrod or move to Las Vegas and he doesn't know what kind of work I've been doing."

"An escort?" Ben asked.

She nodded. "Look, I admit it's not the best decision I've made, but it was between that and working a minimum-wage job. I wasn't going to return home to Florida broke and without Jarrod... well... I would have never been able to live that down. Nah, I had plans. Big plans. A house, a car, and decent job."

"So you thought escorting would get you there faster?"

"I figured six months and I would have enough. And maybe I would, had I not hooked up with Rico."

"Rico?" Zeke asked.

"My old pimp. Now had I gone the route of doing it all myself, via Craigslist and whatnot, like I did in the last two months, I would have easily had enough money to head back out but... that's all in hindsight now."

"And perhaps you would have been dead," Zeke replied. "It's not exactly a friendly city to do that kind of work in."

"No, you're right. Like I said, I didn't plan on being in it this long."

They sat there in silence and Aamir had this confused look on his face.

"So, what does your father do for a living?"

She blurted it out without even giving it a second thought. "He's a teacher at a university but the label most would give him would be an astronomer."

"And so this big important thing that he wanted you to escape from... it wouldn't have been by any chance... an earthquake, would it?"

She looked at him and swallowed. "I would need to check my texts."

"You mean, you didn't look at any of them?" Zeke asked.

"I gazed at a few, but they all seemed pretty much the same. Come home. I miss you. It's not safe. You should leave immediately and so forth. See what you need to understand is that long before I left home he was always paranoid about where I went, and so forth."

Dexter snorted. "But you're a grown woman."

"Exactly!" she exclaimed.

Again there was silence until Aamir piped up.

"Um. I hate to point out the obvious, but wouldn't the part about… it's not safe, have made you check the rest of the texts?"

In her slightly intoxicated mind, she made a face and shrugged.

"You don't know my father."

He leaned in. "Turn on your phone. Check the text messages."

"No point Aamir. I wouldn't be able to get them. They are on a server. They're only displayed once I click on them." She fished out her phone and hit the power. It didn't turn on. "And… there we go, there is no power… great!"

Zeke blew out his cheeks and looked over to Ben. "You know that part about this being a fucked-up situation but it's not that bad as we're not alone?"

Ben raised an eyebrow. "Yeah?"

"Well, I'm questioning the validity of that."

Chapter 9

Over the course of the next hour, they scavenged through the different stores to make sure they had enough to stay strong, safe and alive. There was no way to know how bad it was beyond the hotel. If anyone was alive or if the city had been abandoned?

Aamir wouldn't let up about the phone. He couldn't seem to wrap his head around why Felicity hadn't read all her father's texts. Did he mention an earthquake? How long ago did he send warning messages? What he didn't understand was that her father had always been a little paranoid about where she went due to his work. He'd spent so long staring up into space, keeping an eye out for NEOs, that he'd convinced himself that it was only a matter of time before earth experienced another event like the Cretaceous-Paleogene extinction.

"I can see what you mean. It is a little way out there," Ben muttered as they each stuffed a bag full of snacks, water, knives and batteries from a travel and adventure store.

"Not in his mind. The way my father sees it, it's only a matter of time."

"Hey!" Aamir shouted to them from the back of the store. "I think I've found the solution to our problem."

"Great, is it that extra stack of cash I lost?"

"No, look at this." He held it up, and they aimed their flashlights at it. "It's a portable solar battery charger in a bag."

"Well, that will be of great use to us," Ben muttered. "Now we just need some sun." He chuckled to himself and continued to load up his bag.

"No, that's useful, Aamir," Felicity said trying to make the guy feel good. He was trying to be helpful. She gave Ben a playful slap on the arm, and he grinned.

"You said you clicked on a lot of his texts but didn't read them. If we can get your phone charged up once we get out of here, we can see what he said."

"If we get out of here," Ben added.

Felicity took the bag from him. "Thanks, Aamir."

"You're welcome."

"So continue what you were saying," Ben said as they headed out.

"Around 65 million years ago an asteroid hurtled towards the earth at 45,000 miles an hour. It was six miles wide, estimated to weigh a trillion tons. When it hit, the impact triggered the formation of a mountain range that was taller than Mount Everest."

"It's what wiped out the dinosaurs?"

"You got it. At least that's what they believe."

"How do they know?" Ben asked.

"The K-T boundary, other otherwise known as the K-Pg boundary."

"The what?"

Aamir piped up. "A thin band of rock that was found by paleontologists."

Both Felicity and Ben looked at him.

"You're familiar with the boundary?" Felicity asked.

"Of course." He looked away and then back at them.

"What? You think because I drive a cab that I don't know anything? I went to college. I have a B.A. in history."

"And paleontology?"

"No. I wanted to become a teacher. After I got out, I couldn't seem to land a position. One thing led to another, and I had to make ends meet. I got a job working as a cabbie and well… I guess I never got around to pursuing it."

"Well, Ahab, I have to say that is pretty darn impressive. I underestimated you."

Aamir shook his head and walked off.

"Anyway," Felicity continued, "according to the geological record, the K-Pg event left behind a thin layer of sediment called the K-Pg boundary which can be found in rocks today. This boundary of clay shows high levels of iridium, which is rare in the earth's crust but is abundant in asteroids."

"Hey guys, I think I've found a way out," Dexter shouted. While everyone had been gathering supplies, he was searching for a new route out. Zeke said he had a death wish, crawling through all the rubble. Still, it was a glimmer of hope and right now that was all they were holding on to.

"When I get out of here, I'm going to get myself a large hotdog, with layers of chili over it, and wash it down with a nice beer."

"You've already had enough beer," Dexter said to Zeke.

"Hey, don't kill my dream."

There was a new sense they would be okay as they followed Dexter through another dangerous maze of concrete and twisted metal until finally, they saw it — light at the end of the tunnel.

As the last of them stumbled out of the concrete grave, they looked around expecting to see rescue workers, hoping to hear the shouts of people cheering. But there was nothing. The shock on their faces as they soaked in the sight of the city painted a disheartening picture of their reality.

Fear gripped Felicity as she took in the sight of the

dead, and a city torn up.

There didn't appear to be anyone alive, neither rescue workers nor police officers — hell, Las Vegas didn't even look the same. Though it was warm out, the ground was covered in water, in some areas it was up to their knees. Burst pipes continued to shoot water in every direction. The city was in ruins. Huge sections of the road were lifted up, making it look like a skate park of concrete.

Zeke turned, his eyes scanning the horizon. "Where is everyone?"

There was a stunned look on each of their dusty faces.

"It doesn't make sense. If it was just an earthquake, there would be people out here. If not rescue workers, at least the injured, and others trying to help." The only sound they could hear was running water.

"That depends on how dangerous the area was deemed. The government might have evacuated people. Perhaps they are expecting another hit? It's not like people are just going to stay here."

Zeke hurried away, stumbling over large obstacles in

his path.

“Where are you going?”

“I’ve got to get home,” Zeke said, climbing up onto a platform of concrete

“You probably have no home to go back to.”

“I think we should stick together,” Ben added.

As they argued among themselves, Felicity pulled out her phone and hooked it up to the bag’s solar charger. The solar panel had a red LED to show that the sun was charging the power battery pack. How long it would take to fully charge would depend on the strength of the sunshine. She felt like a fool for ignoring her father’s texts and phone calls. But the guilt and shame she’d experienced in the past had just made it too hard. It was just easier to avoid him than to tell him the truth.

“We should probably get out of the city,” Dexter said.

“My home is here,” Aamir replied. “I need to check on my kids, and my wife.”

“Hey, Zeke, wait up!” Ben shouted hurrying after him. Zeke stopped and turned around.

He wiped a hand across his face. "What?"

"We should stick together. It's not safe being out here alone."

He laughed. "What are you, five years old? I'm a grown man for God's sake."

"But—"

"No buts. I don't know you. You don't know me. It's probably best we all just head our own way. It was great knowing you guys," he said in a sarcastic manner. "But I've got to get back to my life."

"What life?" Dexter hollered.

Felicity was preoccupied with her phone, hoping it would turn on soon. "Dexter, just let him go."

They watched Zeke navigate his way through the rubble. It wasn't easy as large areas of the ground were torn open creating massive crevices that couldn't be crossed. Zeke stopped walking and looked down.

"Shit."

"I told you. It will take you days to get home at this rate. You're going to need our help," Ben said. Zeke turned back and scowled. "Zeke, the fact is we don't know what the hell has happened here, other than what we can see, and we have no idea if there will be another quake."

Zeke ran a hand around the back of his neck and cursed a few times before trying to attempt to go around the large crevice, but it had torn so wide he had no other choice than to head back toward where everyone else was. He returned and Felicity spoke up.

"Look, let's try to help Aamir get back home. From there we can figure out what to do next. At least by then I should have power in this phone and maybe we can get answers."

"Sounds good," Ben said.

Dexter shrugged. "I'm in no hurry to go anywhere."

"Well I am," Zeke said blowing out his cheeks and shaking his head. "All right. Fine, let's head to Aamir's place but after this, we go to mine."

After stumbling over all manner of debris and threading their way through the devastation, they were able to get a better view of what had been destroyed. Many of the cars had fallen into the huge crevices, others were turned over and entire buildings had been brought down. The smell of death lingered in the air. They wandered through the mess for what felt like hours.

"What's the time?" Dexter asked.

Zeke looked at his watch and then tapped it. "Shit. Come on."

"What's the matter?"

"It's still showing the same time from earlier on."

"Aamir, do you have a watch on you?"

He pulled up his dirty sleeve and glanced at it. It was cracked. He held it up to his ear. "It's still ticking. It's working!"

"Well bully for you," Zeke said brushing past him.

"It's a little after three in the afternoon."

As they trudged on in the direction that Aamir had given, they spotted several survivors walking aimlessly through the streets. They were covered from head to toe in dust, and to Felicity, it reminded her of the photos from 9/11.

"Hey!" Zeke called out. They turned and looked back but kept on walking.

"What the hell?"

"Well, at least that answers that. Not everyone is gone."

As they headed north on Las Vegas Boulevard, they saw more people. A look of shock covered their faces. It made sense that not everyone would have died, or fled. Some were picking through the remains of rubble. Searching for loved ones? Trying to clear up? There was no way that this place would be cleared up, soon. Never had she seen a quake this bad. Never had Las Vegas been hit by one this bad.

"You there," Zeke called out to some guy off in the distance. The lone survivor hurried towards them when the ground trembled. At first, it was a minor tremor, but then, as if some large unseen force was shaking the earth, it tore open.

"Zeke!" Ben yelled. His legs wobbled as he was

running and then he vanished. One second he was there, and the next, gone in a cloud of dust. Felicity and the others clung to each other for dear life as they tried to avoid sections of buildings collapsing. A huge plume of dust billowed down the main stretch engulfing them like a giant tidal wave.

Felicity could barely breathe. She was choking and gasping for air even as she pulled her top over her face. It was unclear how long it lasted, as one minute she was standing upright, the next she was knocked unconscious.

Was she dead? Felicity had no idea how long she'd been out only that when she awoke, the memory slipped away — the one of her being eleven years old and getting her first telescope from her father.

"Happy birthday, sweetheart. I know you wanted one. How do you like it?"

She peered through it. "It's perfect, Dad."

"Now you'll always be able to see her. She's one of those shining stars."

Although she knew he was trying to make her feel good, and she went along with it, the fact was her mother was never coming back.

Water splashed on her forehead.

When she came to, Aamir was looming over her.

"Felicity, hey, thank God you are back," he said trying to bring a bottle of water up to her dry, cracked lips. He was holding the back of her head and suggesting that she not move.

"Aamir?"

He mumbled some prayer and using some of the water from the bottle to wipe away the dust from her face.

"You're okay."

She tried to get up, but he told her to stay put as he wasn't sure if there would be another quake.

"Where's Ben? Dexter?"

He shook his head despondently. "I don't know if they are alive or dead."

Chapter 10

When the wall of gray cloud thinned out, they could see everything the quake had destroyed. Before they thought it was bad, but now it was far worse. Buildings that had withstood the first quake were now flattened, crevices were wider and even more in number. The earth had devoured vehicles that had survived the first wave. The sound of car alarms blared.

What was causing all this to happen? Felicity tried to think back to the news, days before. There had been a series of hurricanes off the coast of Florida and several forest fires out in California, but that was the norm. It seemed that every year the shores of America were being rocked by Mother Nature.

All she knew was that she was still alive and that they needed to get out of the city before it was too late. Aamir helped her up, and she wiped at her face. A thick layer of gray dust came off like snakeskin. Once up, they tried to make sense of where they were.

"Aamir," a voice croaked from a short distance away. Ben was trapped under a pile of rubble.

"Just stay here, Felicity, I'll be right back." He hurried over and tried to free Ben but he was trapped below a large slab of concrete. It had caught a portion of his clothing and encased him between two slabs.

Felicity rose and staggered a little until she could find her feet. She searched around for the other two.

"Zeke. Dexter!"

She climbed over more debris that had been turned into small hills. She grabbed hold of a large piece of twisted metal and pulled herself up until she could get a better view.

"Dexter!"

"Felicity!"

That's when she spotted him. He was trapped inside a car turned on its side.

"How the hell did you get in there?"

"When everything crumbled, I landed on top of the car and climbed in through the window." He might have been able to get out but the car itself was balancing on an edge and the moment he shifted his body, it creaked, threatening to drop into a black abyss of fire and smoke. So much of the dirt and rubble had been shoved and lifted that every single water pipe that was buried beneath the roads had burst, creating mini streams full of dirty water.

It was hard to tell what was the roadway and what was the sidewalk, they had been smashed together.

"Hold on, I'll try to find something to get you out."

She climbed down and headed over to Aamir who was still struggling to free Ben.

"We need to find some rope or something to get Dexter out."

"Best of luck, there is nothing here but back in that adventure store, there was some. It was hanging up. I don't think it was for sale, it looked as if it was part of the décor."

She nodded and took off towards the store when Aamir called out.

"Look, I can go get it. You might be searching in there for a while. I know where it is."

She nodded and let him go while she went back to Dexter to tell him to hold on.

"Hold on? Where else can I go?"

As she sat there at the top of a large slab of concrete that had been scooped up, she saw movement just off to her right. The sun was bright and she had to cup a hand over her eyes to block the glare. She spotted a hand, then an arm, then his face. She figured Zeke was dead but sure enough, that was him — alive and well.

"Zeke!"

"I would wave but then I would fall to my death. You want to give me a hand?"

Five minutes later, Zeke was brushing himself off and recounting what happened. "I shouldn't have tried to speak with that man. One second the ground was there, the next it was gone, nothing but a cloud of dust.

Fortunately, I landed on a small ledge."

"The other guy?"

He shrugged. "No idea."

He brushed off some of the dust from his pants. It would be impossible to get rid of it all.

"This day just keeps getting better," he said.

"At least you're alive."

"I'm not sure if that's a good thing or not," Zeke muttered, cracking a weak smile. They headed back across the obstacle course, winding their way around snapped sign poles and twisted iron rebar that stuck out from concrete. While Zeke tried to catch his breath over by Ben, Felicity looked down into the car that was only supported by rebar, and a chunk of concrete. One more quake and Dexter and that vehicle would be gone for good.

Dexter looked like he was playing a game of Twister. He was supporting himself with one hand against the top and had his knees on the side of a headrest. Even the slightest movement caused the vehicle to rock.

"You got a family?"

"What?" Dexter replied.

"Family. When Zeke asked, you didn't respond."

"That's because he's an asshole. I've got a family."

"Yeah, how many?"

He laughed. "Why? Are you going to tell them I was a swell guy when this thing drops and I go with it?"

"You're getting out, Dexter, so you can tell them yourself."

He shook his head and for a second he paused. "That's the thing. Even if this dropped, no one would know, let alone care."

Her brow knit together as she studied him. "Someone would care. Hell, I don't have the best relationship with my father but I know right now if he's still alive, he's probably pulling his hair out trying to find out if I'm okay."

"That's good for you. You should cling to that. I burned my bridges many years ago."

"What do you mean?"

He shook his head. "Oh, it's a long story. It doesn't matter."

She studied his face. "Why do you do that all the time?"

"What?"

"Brush people off because you think they're not interested."

He laughed. "Listen, Felicity, ninety percent of people don't care about your problems or mine as they are too caught up in their own and the ten percent that do, they want you to have them."

"That's a screwed-up view of the world."

"But it's true."

"I don't believe that."

"Look around you. Think about all the devastation that has happened on this planet. In 2014, 700 people died in China after a magnitude-6.2 quake. 2013, 825 died in Pakistan after another quake. 90,000 dead in China after the quake in 2008, 18,000 died in Japan after a 9.0 magnitude in 2011. 700 in 2010 in Chile, and then

316,000 in Haiti all in the same year. Now think about how many times you have thought about those people? How many times have you thought about how you can help the survivors?" he paused. "Right. No one cares."

"That's not true. For someone who says no one cares, you seem to remember a lot of the events you think people have forgotten."

He shook his head and offered a smile before the vehicle creaked again.

She continued to stare at him. "What did you do for a living before this?"

"Does it matter?"

"Humor me."

He sighed. "I was a thief. You satisfied?"

She screwed up her face.

"I stole what I needed to survive on the streets."

"You were homeless?"

He took a moment to reply to that. "Yes."

"You don't have an apartment?"

"No, at least I haven't for the last four years." He

looked up at her. "Would you believe me if I said I used to have a lot of money in the bank? A good job?" He collected himself and she could see he had diverted his eyes because they were welling up. "And a family that cared for me."

"What happened?"

"I blew it. I was a stockbroker. I was raking in the dough and living the high life. But like anything that's pushed to the extreme, I partied too hard, sucked down one too many Jack Daniel's and snorted my way through a mountain of coke." He paused. "Then everything spiraled down. Before I knew it my house and two vehicles were repossessed, and I found myself couch surfing — one night with my family, another with my buddy. Anyway, they soon grew tired of it. After that, I was out on the streets. You soon find out quickly who are your friends. And as for my family, well, that's why I say… no one cares. They say they care but what they really are saying is… Dexter… you are an embarrassment to this family. Dexter… everyone has problems, what makes you any different? Dexter…"

"But you know you brought most of that on yourself?"

He chuckled. "You're preaching to the choir, Felicity. I've already had family and friends tear a limb off me, so go ahead, there isn't much left of me that anyone can take."

"Your family never opened their doors to you even after knowing you were on the street?"

"I never told them."

"So you are out here because of choice?"

"Felicity, 99% of people who are on the streets are here because of their own choices."

"But they might have taken you back in."

"Trust me, Felicity. I know my family. That wouldn't happen."

"Why?"

He shook his head.

A hard wind blew across her cheeks and she coughed from the dust. She pulled off her backpack and wiped away the dust from the solar panels and checked to make sure that the unit was still working and charging. It was.

"Hey!" Zeke shouted over. "How's that thief doing?"

She looked down at Dexter and he squeezed his eyes shut.

"Did you not try to get another job?"

"Of course. I've done many jobs but it's hard to hold them down when you are feeding an addiction."

She chewed over what he was saying. "That's why, isn't it? You stole from them?"

He laughed a little and then blew his cheeks out. "Like I said, addiction is hard."

"And that's why you couldn't go back."

"Don't sound so surprised. I mean, let's face it. You aren't much better than me."

She bristled. "I didn't mean it like that."

"Yeah, well, if it's so easy to return to family, why are you not answering your father's texts?"

She swallowed and looked away. "I'm going to see if Aamir has got back."

"Yeah, you do that."

Felicity slipped down the large slab of concrete and chewed over what he had told her. She wasn't trying to make him feel bad and yet, she wondered if that's how everyone reacted when they heard about someone's life not fitting the norm — the norm being, holding down a regular 9 to 5 job, being married and not using drugs. She was the last person to point the finger. Much like him, her own choices had got her to where she was, and if she was honest, there had been times she had been close to being homeless.

"Guys! I got it."

Aamir came rushing back holding this thick rope in his hand. It looked like something straight out of the Wild West, the kind of rope that might have been used to lasso cattle. With all that had happened, Aamir was the only one that had a smile on his face. For someone who worked as a cabbie and probably worked harder than any of the others, his attitude was different, it was unusual, refreshing even.

A few minutes later, the rope was lowered down into

the vehicle and Dexter took a firm hold of it.

"Remember. The moment I push off, pull me up."

"We won't leave you hanging," Aamir said. Dexter gave Felicity this look as if he was trying to communicate just with his eyes, perhaps wondering what she thought about what he'd told her. It took all three of them, and one part of the rope was tied around some rebar.

"Go!"

Dexter pushed off and metal groaned as he yelled for them to pull him up. Slowly but surely he climbed and each of them put their back into it to hold him until he made it over the lip of concrete.

He let out a deep sigh and took a second to catch his breath. He chuckled from relief but it was cut short at the sound of the car giving way. Felicity hurried over to the edge just in time to see it disappear into the chasm below. It smashed against the side and then was gone. A huge billow of dust rose, and she took a few steps back.

Felicity extended her hand to Dexter. He looked at it and grabbed a hold.

"You know, that's all great and all, but a little help!" Ben shouted and Aamir laughed. They didn't imagine getting him out would be harder than rescuing Dexter but it was. It took all four of them, every ounce of strength they had to free him. They wedged snapped-off pieces of metal under the slab of concrete.

"Come on, push."

One second they thought they had it, the next they had to let go, and it came down hard. Each time it got closer and closer to pressing against Ben's actual body. Sweat was pouring off their brows, and Zeke had taken off his coat, rolled up his sleeves and was going red in the face.

Dexter groaned, putting everything he had into it. Felicity crouched down and took a hold of Ben's arms. "Okay on three. One, two, three!" she yelled, and they worked the metal under the slab and pulled down as she tugged at his sleeves.

Suddenly, they did it. His clothing pulled away, and she could slide him out with the help of Aamir. Once he was out, the other two collapsed on top of him out of pure exhaustion.

"Next time…" Aamir started.

"There won't be a next time," Ben muttered.

That was one thing they could agree on, at least for now. Reality was they didn't know if the danger was over or just beginning.

Chapter 11

Charlie was guided into a large control center in the heart of the underground base of Cape Canaveral. NASA employees worked feverishly to ensure that the exodus of a hundred thousand people to the International Space Station *Deliverance* would happen without a glitch. All the power in the base came from generators, they even had their own means of communicating through a system that didn't rely on the main power grid.

"*Deliverance*. That's what they are calling it?" Charlie asked looking up at the large screen which provided updates in real time and video footage of those already on board from nations all over the world.

"It was a joint effort."

"When did they build this?"

"Long before we got your warning. They built it in space, decades ago in preparation for an event like this and interstellar travel."

"I guess next you will tell me that's possible?"

"Yes, and no. They have been rotating teams up in space and extending the period that each team is onboard. What you are looking at here is state-of-the-art technology. Few people on this planet even know about this. All those billions of dollars in black budget money," he tapped the screen. "That's where it's gone."

He swiped a screen and rotated the airship. It was like something out of a sci-fi movie. It resembled four huge hamster wheels with a sleek ship at the center attached to the outer rings by spokes. "It has everything, Charlie. Artificial gravity, kitchens, cockpit, medical and science labs, living and working quarters, cargo storage, observation rooms, hibernation pods, eating areas, a shopping mall, escape modules and much more. The thing is powered by nuclear fission generators and it has ionized plasma drive."

"That's fantastic, William, but without my daughter it means nothing."

"Look, I know it's hard."

“Do you? Let me guess, your wife and kids are on that list?”

William pursed his lips. He didn’t need to reply to that as Charlie knew it was true. There was no way in hell he would have gone up without them.

“How long ago did you get your family on that list?” He paused. “Actually don’t even bother answering that.”

William put his arm around Charlie. “Listen, let me show you some of the airships that will take us up.” He led Charlie out and continued to discuss the advancements that NASA had made. They were in many ways light years ahead, and in others far behind. All the best technology had been reserved for government usage and what William kept stating was for the continuity of government. Through mammoth steel jaws, he was led into a launch bay where technicians and engineers had been working around the clock to ensure that the launch ships would be ready to leave within four days. That was the estimated time of when the asteroid would hit earth.

“By the time that rock hits, we will be far away from

the earth. Anything and everything on this planet will be destroyed."

"I already know that," Charlie said as he continued to drone on.

The impact of the one that had wiped out 75% of the earth's population 65 million years ago had released 6 million times the energy of the 1980 eruption of Mount St. Helens. The destruction of every living thing occurred in stages. First, the super-heated gases and debris incinerated everything around the impact zone. Nothing inside a 1,000-mile radius would have survived. As the asteroid landed in the water, it created a tidal wave and sent up red-hot debris that put into effect a chain of events that not only wiped out the dinosaurs but set the stage for the next evolution of mankind.

As William stood there pointing out various features on the ship and acting like a wild-eyed kid, Charlie's mind thought back to the lecture he'd given at the University of Florida only two years prior. He had stood before numerous students, some of whom doubted that an asteroid could wipe out the planet.

"At the point of impact, the temperature would have been around 8,000 degrees. It would have melted the surrounding rock and shot out molten bullets at supersonic speed. The earth would have experienced super-heated 2,000 miles an hour winds. Literally, it would have been like hell on earth." He scribbled on the whiteboard. "The initial shockwave would have created a tsunami across Mexico, crashing into Georgia, Alabama and the western side of America. The wall of the tsunami would have been ten times higher than the one in 2004 which was thirty feet high. This 300-foot wall would have hurtled out at hundreds of miles an hour."

A student muttered something, and he made a gesture with his head.

"You have a question?"

"I was just wondering how likely it would be that this could happen again?"

"Our job is not to wonder if it will happen but determine when it will happen. And believe me, unless we are ready,

which we are not, life as we know it will be over, just as it was back then. After the super-heated fireball heated the earth's atmosphere, the devastation would have reached around the world and would have been incredible. We know this to be true as we found small parts of soot and charcoal in the layer which shows all the vegetation went up in flames and suggests there was a global inferno."

Charlie then had one of them shut off the lights so he could turn on the overhead projector and play a clip of Los Alamos scientists in the applied physics division using supercomputers to study the impact. He stood back against the wall as it played out and a 3D simulation showed the students the KT impact. He interjected to explain what they were seeing.

"It would have been so powerful that 5 billion tons of debris would have hurled into the air. This would have gone up into the upper atmosphere, then into space and orbited causing it to land elsewhere on the earth. As this debris rained down, it would have caused the atmosphere to heat to where there would have been forest fires from spontaneous

combustion. On the far side of the world, the wildfires would have been lethal."

He stared around at the crowd of students, many of whom were his daughter's age.

"So, such an event would cause a sudden and dramatic climate change. Dust, debris, and ash in the atmosphere would have been so thick it would have made it night for at least three months. You wouldn't have been able to see your hand in front of your face for close to six months."

A student's hand shot up.

"I don't get it. Why?"

"Because the dust and ash would block out the sun." He stepped forward and changed the image to a new one showing droplets. "The vaporized rock would contain sulfur dioxide and when combined with the water in the atmosphere it would have created sulfuric acid droplets. Now, what do we know about that? Well, it would have caused temperatures to plummet. You see at first dust would have blocked out the sun, then it would fall back to earth and slowly over time get cleaned out. However, these sulfur

oxides in the upper atmosphere would have reflected the sunlight and cooled the planet, essentially throwing it into a state of winter for several years. Temperatures would drop to around 5 degrees Celsius. Forests that had been destroyed would struggle to regenerate. Eventually, this sulfur dioxide would fall as acid rain. So, there would be six months of winter when there was no sunlight at all, and then when the planet gets a little sunlight after that, the plants think they can grow again, only to get acid rain killing them off."

"Sir, are you saying that nothing would have survived? Because if nothing survived, how come we are here today?"

"I'm getting to that. The few animals that would have survived the initial blast, the tsunami, the wildfires and the plummeting temperatures would soon starve. Essentially the asteroid would have a domino effect. Global cooling would make way for global warming because the rocks that the asteroid hit didn't just contain sulfur, they contained carbon dioxide, which released greenhouse gas of the equivalent of 3,000 years of modern fossil fuel burning. This continued for centuries. Even the toughest plants would have died, and

herbivores, which relied on these, would have died along with the carnivores. Still, even though the KT impact wiped out 70% of the species on the planet, a few survived— mammals — small ones that burrowed underground. These omnivores could eat plants or meat. Now you might ask yourself, okay then, why did the dinosaurs not survive but these small mammals did? Well, from what we know, these mammals were shielded from the heat of the blast by using burrows or aquatic environments. Once the heat was gone, they came back out and could use what remaining food resources had survived. Now that might not have been enough for dinosaurs but for small mammals, it seems so. And before you ask… why did some mammals survive and others didn't? Well, that is still a mystery, and scientists are still trying to gather evidence to answer this question."

"Charlie. Charlie!" William repeated his name, and he snapped back into the present moment. "I thought I had lost you there."

"Just preoccupied."

"So what do you think?"

"I think I need to find my daughter."

Charlie turned and headed for the door when William caught up. "You can't possibly be entertaining the thought of going out there?"

"I need to find her, otherwise all of this has been for nothing."

"It's not for nothing, Charlie. Thousands of lives will be saved. Humanity will go on."

"I made a promise."

He walked away.

"This is about her, isn't it? Kathy."

Charlie stopped walking and turned back. "I couldn't look at myself in the mirror if I knew Felicity was still out there alive. I made a promise to her I would do everything I could to make sure she was looked after."

"She's not a child anymore, Charlie."

"No. No, she's not. But that doesn't mean I care for her any less."

He stood there staring at William. William drew

closer. "Look, I can speak to one of the generals and see if there is anything we can do, but it's not safe to be out there. Besides, we need you here."

"For what? There's nothing left to do. Anything that could have been done, should have been done by now, instead, the government has cherry-picked who will live and die, and withheld vital information that could have saved more lives."

William put a hand on his hip and shook his head. "It wouldn't have saved lives, Charlie, and you know that. What the hell would you expect them to do?"

"Give them some kind of warning."

He stepped a little closer. "You've watched one too many movies, my friend. That's not how it works. It would send people into a state of panic. Thousands would riot. There would be mass deaths. Why? Because nobody would have anything to lose. At least this way we get to save some. I'm sorry, Charlie, that it's not the way you saw it playing out, but it is what it is."

Charlie shook his head.

"Just consider yourself lucky that I made the call to have your name put on the list. So leave this with me. I'll go speak with one of the military officials and maybe, just maybe I might have good news for you. Until then, hang tight, go get yourself a coffee. It's gonna be okay."

"I hope so."

Chapter 12

The smell of death lingered in the air. From what they could tell, over twenty-four hours had expired since the initial earthquake. In the dry heat of Vegas, with temperatures hovering somewhere up around 100 Fahrenheit, it hadn't taken long for the bodies to decompose. The smell was like a combination of rotting eggs, feces and mothballs. All of them covered the lower half of their faces with cloth torn from their clothing. Though Felicity had got one bar of power on the phone, she didn't want to turn it on until it was at least halfway charged. Just hearing it ding gave her a sliver of hope.

What should have taken only forty minutes to reach Aamir's home proved to be much harder than they expected. The apartments were on the northwest side. Wide crevices prevented them from taking a direct route, so they were forced to work their way around uneven areas of ground, leap across divided stretches and even do a balancing act across downed road signs. Not every area was knee-deep in water, but with so many water mains having burst, the roads or what was left of them had been turned into mini rivers.

"I don't get why it's continuing to pump out, wouldn't it stop flowing once the power shut off?" Zeke muttered.

"Backup generators. Many of these large companies operate them in the event of power loss. They have to have them. It won't be long though and it will eventually cut out," Aamir said.

Felicity's feet sloshed through deep water, every step felt as dangerous as the last because the water wasn't clear. There was no way of telling if her next step would cause her to sink, or twist an ankle. She kept moving using a piece of broken pipe to test the ground ahead of her.

"You sure we are heading in the right direction?" Ben asked.

Dexter glanced at the small compass on the back of Felicity's backpack. "Seems so."

"What happens if they are dead?"

Aamir looked at him and his chin dropped. There was a strong possibility that none of them had survived. The devastation was so wide, it would have been a miracle.

As they came over a huge rise, they stopped walking and looked on at a plane, or what remained of it. Its charred bones lay scattered across the street. It wasn't one of the large airliners but looked to be a private jet.

No words were shared between them but it was clear by the expression on their faces they were all thinking similar things. Felicity looked behind her towards the Luxor to see how far they had come and then shook her head. "We have been walking for close to thirty minutes and we have barely made it a few blocks. At this rate, we will reach your apartment by evening."

Felicity pressed a hand against her back and stretched out. She was sore, her muscles were aching and there were several cuts on her arms and face from the fall.

"You think we can rest up?" Ben asked. "My leg is killing me."

She wandered over and noticed that the lower half was drenched in blood.

"You mind?" Felicity asked. He shrugged. She pulled up his pant leg, and he winced, and that's when she saw the damage. It wasn't just bruised, it looked as if the whole thing had swollen up.

"We need to get some water on that and clean it before it gets infected."

Felicity yelled to the others as they were still pressing on. "Guys, hold up."

They stopped and looked back.

Ben hobbled to a slope of concrete and gripped a piece of thick rebar. Felicity pulled off her bag and pulled out a bottle of water she'd taken from the hotel shops. She twisted off the cap and poured it over his leg. He groaned.

"Really?"

"It hurts," he muttered.

"I'm no doctor but that thing is looking like you might have a break as its swelling up like a balloon."

He slammed his fist against the concrete. "Great. Real

great!"

Dexter stumbled over. "What's going on?" he asked just as he took in the sight of Ben's leg. "Oh, I wish I hadn't asked. That is gnarly. Why didn't you tell us?"

"Because..."

"He's a martyr," Zeke said shaking his head and looking out across the mounds of debris.

"I'm sorry, Aamir, you'll have to go ahead without us. We need to get his leg up and do DIY on this thing."

"DIY?"

"Well, you don't want it getting any worse."

"You're not a doctor."

She shrugged. "It's up to you. We can leave you here or maybe we can head to the nearest hotel that is still intact and looked for a med kit." She cupped a hand over her eyes and looked off into the distance. "The Mirage is not far from here. I say we head over there."

He nodded and looked up at Aamir. "Sorry, my friend."

"Nothing to be sorry about."

"I don't want to slow you up."

"Yeah, you can continue without us," Zeke said, a smile lingering on his face. He didn't want to head to Aamir's home. That was obvious. "I say we head to the hotel and get out from this heat. At least find something to eat."

"What happened to the snacks in your bag?"

"I ate them."

They all stared at him.

He shrugged. "What? I was hungry."

Dexter stepped in and put Ben's arm around the back of his neck. "Come on, Zeke, give me a hand."

"Carry him?"

"Well, he isn't going to walk much farther with his leg chewed up like that."

"Shit," he muttered before reluctantly going over to his right side and helping him up. Ben groaned in pain. "I don't know what you're groaning about, you're not the one carrying you. What are you? Two hundred and forty pounds?"

"Stop bellyaching," Dexter said.

The last forty minutes had been full of stopping and starting, but now it was taking even longer. Felicity led the way picking the least challenging route. She wiped sweat from her brow and gazed up into the sky at the blistering sun. She downed what little remained in the water bottle and ran some of it over her head. Droplets of water ran off her, cooling her down, if only for a few minutes.

They assumed they would see more people but there were none.

Of course, that didn't mean there weren't any. Many of them were probably trapped inside hotels, stuck under rubble or making their way out of the city.

"I'm thinking a bunch of folks evacuated in those first twenty-four hours, and those that remained were probably swallowed up by the earth."

They pressed on wading through more water, water that was not only coming from burst pipes but the huge swimming pool outside the Polynesian-themed resort and casino. The Mirage was a mammoth hotel on the Las Vegas strip that had over 3,000 rooms. While one whole section of the hotel had collapsed, the other part was still standing though there were no windows. All the glass had been shattered. The palm trees that once were dotted around the pool in front of the hotel were now gone. In their place was a huge crevice.

As they made their way inside to where visitors would have registered, it was a chaotic scene. The marble floors were cracked and heaved up. Light fixtures and chandeliers were on the ground, smashed into hundreds of pieces, and tables and chairs overturned. A large section of the ceiling had collapsed exposing drywall, and all manner of electrical wires.

Smoke billowed out from an area farther down the hall where a fire crackled away. Mangled sprinkler pipes had ceased to pump out water.

There was no one inside, at least alive.

However, the smell of death was potent.

"Okay, turn that couch up and lay him down there,"

Felicity said. There was a fancy red-and-gold couch in a waiting area. It had a thick layer of dust.

Ben winced as they tried to make him comfortable.

"I'll go look for a first-aid kit," Dexter said. "You want to give me a hand?" he asked Zeke.

"Me? I just carried him. My back is aching. I'm taking a breather."

Dexter shook his head and walked off.

Felicity pulled up a chair close to him and checked her phone to see how much power there was before deciding to leave the bag just out front so it could sit in the sun and keep charging. When she returned, Aamir was over by the front desk rooting around.

"Cookies!" he cried out like an overly enthusiastic child.

It was common in hotels in Vegas. They would hand out warm cookies to guests as they arrived. Some provided a cool bottle of water, others nothing unless there was a price tag attached to it.

Felicity had just taken a seat beside Ben when Aamir

called out to them, “Hey guys, guys! I have a dial tone.”

“What?” Ben responded. “That’s impossible, it requires power.”

Dexter suddenly appeared off to the left. “No, actually it doesn’t. Well sort of. Think back to whenever you have had a power outage. Your landline continues to operate because it requires a low voltage, it uses dedicated copper wires that connect to the phone and the power is sent through the phone line from the power company. And, like Aamir said earlier about the water system, most power companies work off a battery backup and backup generators to ensure operations can keep working for well over a week if needed. Eventually though it will stop.”

“Are you kidding me?” Felicity said getting up and heading over towards the phone. “How the hell do you know this?”

“I thought everyone knew it. Back when they had that big hurricane, there was an article that came out about how one woman had to walk a mile and a half from her home to police just to tell them that her grandmother had passed away. She said she had tried her phone, but it didn't work. That's because she was using a cell. Not all cell towers have backup generators and those that do, only work for around four to six hours. Oh, and they aren't designed for a mass of people calling at once which is what would have happened when this shit storm kicked off. Eventually they give up the ghost. But landlines, that's technology that will work for a while. Now again that all depends on the phone company keeping their generators running."

Zeke shoved Dexter against the wall and grabbed him by the throat. "Are you telling me I could have called someone back at the hotel?"

"Hey!" Felicity yelled heading over to get between them.

She didn't need to intervene; Dexter pushed him back and jabbed his finger in his face. "I didn't see a phone and you didn't ask. And even if there was one, that doesn't mean it would have worked. The lines run underground and everything has been heaved up. The fact that this one is working is a miracle. So get off my back."

"A thief and an idiot."

"Fuck you, Zeke."

While this was all going on, Aamir had been trying to call 911 but was getting no response, he then tried his home but again got nothing. Zeke would have been next but Aamir handed the phone to Felicity. "Ladies before slimeballs," he said narrowing his gaze. Felicity felt hope rise in her chest as she dialed the number for her father.

"Come on, pick up, pick up."

It rang several times before the voicemail took over. "Shit!" she muttered.

She almost burst out crying when she heard her father's prerecorded voice on the other end. It beeped and her mind went blank. She hadn't spoken to her father in such a long time. What little communication they had came by way of text or email. Even though she would only leave a message, she was choked up and could barely speak.

"Dad, it's me, I'm alive." She felt her eyes welling up.

"If you hear this, I'm in Las Vegas. This place got hit real bad. There's me and four others here that have survived. I don't know what's going on or if you're even alive but if you hear this, I need help. We need help. I'm scared and well, I'll try to make it back to Florida but I don't know if—"

The line cut off.

She closed her eyes and put it back on the hook.

"You done?" Zeke asked. She nodded, at least for now.

Ben looked over and studied her face as a few tears streaked down her cheek.

"I would say it will be okay but I really don't know. Are you serious about trying to make your way back to Florida?" He paused. "That's over two thousand miles away."

"I should have listened to my father. He must have known about this. He warned me about something big happening but I don't think he was at liberty to say what it was."

"When?"

"A year ago. That's when he started acting all paranoid and sending me texts on a weekly basis. Before that, we hadn't spoken in close to two years."

There was silence between them.

"Do you mind me asking why?"

She wiped away tear streaks. "Just the way he handled my mother in her final years before she died of cancer. He was always working. Always had a reason he couldn't pull away. I think he thought my mother would just bounce back. She went into remission but then it came back, and spread. I told him he needed to drop everything but that's not my father. He said after, I mean after she died that it was his way of dealing with it. That my mother wouldn't have wanted him to see her like that but that was bullshit."

From behind her, she could hear Zeke swearing, then he smacked the phone against the wall in frustration before Aamir pried it out of his hands.

"Are you stupid?"

Zeke mumbled something and walked off. He hadn't

been getting anywhere with whoever he was trying to contact. Like her, he left a message for what sounded like his manager but that was it — they were alone and the only ones that could help them now were themselves.

Chapter 13

He staggered back, gripping his forehead at the sound of her voice. Charlie was on his third cup of coffee when he used one of the landline phones to check his voicemail. He stood there in a cafeteria, staring at the steady stream of people as his daughter's words sank in. In the underground base he felt like a fish out of water watching FEMA officials and NASA employees running back and forth. He'd seen several Black Hawks land and had spoken with doctors, nurses, engineers and those who held prominent positions. They were the elite, the ones who could be counted on to contribute. The ones that troops were saving. They were the ones on the list. The government didn't want to waste the valuable resources and seats on those who would be nothing but a burden.

He'd seen the list, gone through some of the names and job descriptions. It wasn't like it was a shock. The government had first created the contingency plan during the Cold War. Its goal, first and foremost, was to protect the highest-ranking officials in government. It outlined evacuation procedures, bunker locations, airborne command posts, armored command trains, the floating White House, how to secure precious documents from the National Archives through to detailed instructions for the continuation. Washington had even created a dedicated helicopter squadron, code-named "MUSSEL," specifically for evacuating high-ranking officials.

"Charlie."

He heard William's voice but didn't respond until he said it again. Charlie looked up from his seat, and William placed his hand on his shoulder.

"I spoke with one of the captains in charge of the Marines. Unfortunately, he said they can't risk a mission when first off they don't know where your daughter is and secondly because it's a liability."

"I know where my daughter is."

"Vegas, I know but they need specifics. Do you know the extent of the damage out there? What are we dealing with? That first quake was just the beginning of several more. They haven't seen back-to-back quakes like this in, well, a long time and definitely not of this magnitude."

"William, she left a message on my machine. She's at the Mirage."

"I'm sorry, Charlie. I don't know what to say. The team is already being pushed to the limit with the collection of those on the evacuation list. It's just not a priority right now."

Charlie rose from his seat. He could feel his collar tightening, and his blood boiling. "A priority? If it wasn't for the alert I gave, you folks wouldn't have even created the *Deliverance*."

"I told you, they began work on that long before we received the notification. It's been in the works for some time. And besides, NASA would have spotted it, eventually."

"You owe me, William."

He scrunched up his face. "Owe you? If anyone owes anything, it's you. You were not on the list. I got you on there." He studied Charlie's face. "Now you're lucky they haven't gone through that with a fine-tooth comb, otherwise you and I might have been turfed out of this bunker."

"Please, William, all I need is one Black Hawk and two Marines."

"They won't listen."

"Who won't? Introduce them to me. Perhaps I can get them to listen."

"Enough, Charlie!" He said it so loud that people in the cafeteria turned and stared. William lowered his voice and took a seat across from him. Charlie slowly sat down and clasped his hands together. "I can't go then."

"What?"

"I'm not going up if she doesn't come with me. I couldn't live with myself knowing that she was on earth when that asteroid hits."

William sighed and shook his head. "You are killing me here, Charlie." He glanced off towards the doors that separated the cafeteria from the rest of the underground complex. "If I can get what you need, you have to make sure that there is confirmation that your daughter is still there. When was the phone message left?"

"Two hours ago."

"Did she leave a number? Have you tried phoning the Mirage?"

"It was the first thing I did. There was no answer."

"So you want me to stick my neck out on the line, risk the lives of Marines by sending them to a location that you are unsure if she is even there?"

Charlie's eyebrows rose and William clenched his jaw. The muscles tightened and Charlie knew he was pushing his luck but he had nothing to lose.

"And I want to go with them."

William ran a hand over his face. "No. That's not happening."

"It's my daughter."

"Losing two Marines would be hard but losing someone like yourself. We need your expertise. Leave this with me and in the meantime, try again to contact that hotel." He shook his head. "I can't believe that the phone is even working."

"Backup generators. But I doubt it will last. One more quake and that line might be torn up. That's why we need to act immediately."

William got up and drummed his knuckles against the table. "Stay here, I'll be right back."

Charlie leaned back in his seat and felt a wave of hope. There was no guarantee he would convince them, that's why he planned on speaking with them directly. He watched William head towards the door and once he was through, he followed him. Even though everyone knew an asteroid was on its way to earth, the morale inside that bunker was high. How could it not be? All their lives would be saved. A small sliver of society would live on, high above the earth in space for three or more years until earth would be habitable again. As he followed William, he remembered having the discussion with William several years before that. At that time, he hadn't been at liberty to share that information but in a roundabout way, he'd clarified that the government was ready even if the rest of the world wasn't. It seemed selfish to think a tiny portion of society would live on while the rest died but the cost and magnitude of trying to save seven billion people wasn't feasible or practical. It all came down to the needs of the few outweighed the needs of the many.

In the distance he watched William place his hand on a vertical scanner before a door slid open and he went in. Charlie moved fast, making sure to slip in on his coattails. He hadn't seen the entire base since his arrival. Some areas including this one were off-limits to him. Both of them had just entered a large control room with hundreds of computers and a map of the world. Certain areas were blinking, and clusters of people stood around discussing issues related to the launch. There were multiple viewing screens that showed video footage from different countries. The USA wasn't the only country that had a contingency plan, nor was the *Deliverance* only going to hold those from the Western world. It was an international joint effort — one that would ensure the survival of officials from every country in the world.

William approached three military officers and began talking. Charlie was too far back to hear what they were saying but one of them was shaking his head. He could see William jabbing his finger. He had that same look on his face that he had way back in college. He knew it all too well. Now whether it went against his better judgment or not, Charlie made a beeline for the group and interrupted them. He came from behind William and placed a hand on his back.

"I'm sorry, William, but preferential treatment is not—"

"Gentlemen. I'm Charlie Meyer." He extended his hand and greeted them. They all looked surprised and one of them stared down at his badge, no doubt to see if he had clearance. Charlie just got straight to it. "Look, I'm not going to cherry coat this or try to make this palatable. You all have families. You all understand the gravity of this situation. And whether you have been informed or not, the reason you are all going to live is because I was the one who spotted DA29 a year ago. Does that mean I deserve to have special treatment? That's for you to decide. However, I would pose this question to you. If it was your son, daughter or family member out there, would you want someone to collect them?"

They all looked a little embarrassed, maybe because they had been caught off guard.

"William," an officer said, as if he was hoping William would pull Charlie aside.

Fortunately, William did nothing and allowed Charlie to continue.

"If you can't give me Marines, at least give me one pilot and I will go myself."

Silence fell over them as the three military officials looked at each other. They asked for a moment of privacy. William pulled Charlie to one side. "What part of stay, did you not get?"

Charlie squeezed William's shoulder. "Hope for the best…"

"… expect the worst," William said, finishing what

they always said to each other while going through college.

Several minutes passed before one officer came over. He nodded. "If you have the coordinates, we will deploy a two-man team but that's it. You get a pilot and another Marine."

"One other thing, sir."

"William, do I need to remind you?"

Charlie wasn't sure what he was referring to, but he figured that it wasn't the first time William had overstepped the line.

"No, sir. Thank you."

He shook his hand, and they parted ways.

"Report to docking bay B. A Black Hawk will leave in ten minutes."

As they walked away, Charlie was curious. "What were you going to ask him?"

"My mother is in a nursing home in Dallas. I thought being as the Hawk would be flying that way they could stop off and collect her."

"Judy never made the list?"

"There are only so many resources available. We all have wives and kids, some have bigger families than others. Everyone has had to make sacrifices."

"But you are the backbone of this operation. Without you, this whole shit show falls apart."

"Not exactly, Charlie."

"Listen, William, our entire careers we have done nothing by the book. We've bent the rules because, without doing it, disasters would have happened. We have paid our dues. And for that, we deserve to get a little something back."

"Drop it, Charlie. Just be thankful they are willing to collect Felicity."

He shook his head. William knew what he was getting at.

"Which reminds me, any luck getting through again?"

"I didn't try."

"Well keep trying. Let's hope it's not too late, and this trip isn't for nothing."

William parted ways with him and his head was downcast. Judy Baxley had been an anchor in William's life. If it wasn't for her, he would have never made it through college, hell, he wouldn't have been alive. Contrary to what most perceived, William was not always as steadfast as he appeared. His father had died in a car crash when he was eleven, he'd lost his eldest brother at sixteen to a drug overdose and he'd nearly followed down the same path. It was only because of his mother he'd managed to pull his life back together and achieve the illustrious career in NASA that others coveted.

Charlie knew how much Judy meant to him. Though she was in her early seventies and had lived a full life, leaving her behind would stay with him for the rest of his days.

And yet how many others were having to do the same?

Not everyone could go.

Not everyone would live.

There was a cost to ensuring the continuation of humanity, and only those who would live to tell the tale would know the full extent. A wave of guilt washed over him. He had just assumed that she was one of those on the list.

Chapter 14

They stared at what remained of the structure. The nine-story block of apartments had been reduced to rubble. Nothing had been spared. It was a pitiful sight to see Aamir clambering over stone crying out the names of his wife and kids. Felicity felt a heaviness in her chest unlike anything she'd ever experienced. In her time working as an escort there had been some serious low points; moments she had contemplated taking her life because the future looked bleak. Yet it didn't compare to this. It didn't even come close. She wasn't sure what stung the most — the thought of her own demise or of those she barely knew?

She'd watched news broadcasts on TV and read the newspapers about quakes. The headlines were always going for the shock factor. They were never ones to gloss over the loss of life. It was always center stage, the hook for getting that next click, getting someone to toss money down and buy a paper.

Hearing about strangers losing their lives was devastating, but she always felt removed from it. Were others the same? Oh, that is terrible, she would think and then click away without another thought. Not that she lacked empathy; it was that she didn't know the people and she was so far removed from the situation it just didn't seem real.

However, now as she watched Aamir sobbing his heart out, she couldn't help feel his pain. Sure, in theory, he was still a stranger but in the small number of hours they had known each other, she could already feel a bond forming. What was that? Her father would often quote the saying, *a stranger is just a friend you haven't met yet.* She cast a glance at the other three. Their lives had collided just as meteors had hit the earth — sudden and unexpected.

Though they knew his family was dead, for the sake of Aamir each of them took the time to call out the names of his kids. Each one stuck in her throat. The more she called out, the closer she came to breaking down.

Eventually, Dexter placed a hand on Aamir's shoulder and told him the words he refused to accept.

"They're gone, Aamir. I'm sorry."

He was on his knees shaking his head and though sitting there would not get them any closer to safety, they stayed with him for another hour, sharing in his grief.

At some point Aamir either accepted it or he no longer wanted to torture himself by staying there as he got up and told the rest of them he was ready to leave.

That brought them to the next stage of their journey — heading for Zeke's home.

This was when things reached a boiling point.

"How much farther?" Dexter asked for the fourth time. The sun's sweltering rays were merciless as a dry heat bore down on them.

"Not far. Just beyond those buildings."

"You've said that for the past twenty minutes. Give us an address."

Zeke cleared his throat. "Well, you know, it's just on

the outskirts of the city."

"That part we understand, how far on the outskirts?"

Dexter had a point. Vegas covered a vast amount of ground and before the quakes, traveling from one side to the other could take forever, especially with the traffic, but now with all the surrounding devastation? A twenty-minute distance could take closer to an hour because of all the rubble and crevices. Some areas were impassible. But they weren't just dealing with that, Ben still had a bad leg. It was a miracle they could make it to Aamir's home with him.

After getting him cleaned up at the Mirage hotel, they figured he'd just badly bruised the leg, and possibly experienced a hairline fracture. There were no bones sticking out and though it was painful, he said he could walk on it if they could create some form of crutches. They couldn't find anything like that but they were able to create a makeshift walking stick from a mop found in a utility room.

"That's it, I'm done. I'm not walking another step

until you give us an address," Dexter said before taking a seat on an upheaved portion of the road.

"I agree," Ben added, hobbling behind.

Zeke looked worried. He pointed in the direction he'd given countless times hoping that everyone would just keep on going but they were all on the same page — without an address, it was just some vague destination.

"Just spit it out, Zeke," Felicity said.

Aamir remained quiet; he hadn't said a thing since leaving.

"Okay, it's on Club Vista Drive in Henderson."

Dexter's brow furrowed. "Henderson?"

Henderson was a city located just on the outskirts of Las Vegas. It butted up against the city and was around 16 miles southeast. Essentially, on a good day using a car, someone could reach there in less than thirty minutes. Except they didn't have a car, they were on foot and facing one of the worst natural disasters in the history of Las Vegas.

"It's about thirty minutes."

"In a car!" Dexter spat. "Walking could take us five hours or more."

"Nonsense, it's just…"

"If you say it's just over there one more time, I'm gonna knock your teeth out."

Zeke scowled at him. "I'd like to see that," he said.

Dexter got up and Felicity was quick to get between them. She placed her hand on Dexter and pushed him back.

"Enough. This isn't helping."

He slapped away her hand. The heat was getting the best of all of them.

"Look, Zeke, he has a point. With Ben's leg, the lack of supplies and this heat, that's a lot to ask of us."

"Fine. I'll go by myself. But I'm telling you all. Staying here in the city is a big mistake. I own a 22,000-square-foot estate. A mountaintop mansion I'm sure is still there."

"Sure? That's what I thought," Aamir spoke up for the first time. He lifted his chin. "You want us to walk five hours towards something that might just be fragments of stone? You are more insane than I thought."

Zeke narrowed his eyes. "I don't need this shit. You want to stay here, be my guest."

With that said he turned and marched away until he stumbled over a section of rebar, to which Dexter let out a chuckle. "Yeah, good luck with that. You're liable to break your neck before you make it a mile."

Zeke scowled, picked himself up off the ground and brushed off the dust before continuing on.

"We should follow," Felicity said.

"Hell no, he's had people following him all his career. Doing what he says, getting him what he wants. Let him figure this out on his own."

"I'm not saying we should go to his home, I'm just saying he's not thinking clearly and…"

"You think he needs us?" Dexter asked cutting her off. "As he looks like he's dealing with things just fine."

They sat there for a while watching Zeke struggle to climb over areas of debris and weave his way around overturned vehicles and large sections of monuments. It would take him a long time before he disappeared out of view. There was just too much devastation. A huge monorail used to transport guests from hotels to shops had collapsed.

Not far from where they sat was a dead woman draped over concrete, her head crushed, just the lower half of her body sticking out. Was she a tourist or a local? Was anyone searching for her? Las Vegas wasn't empty. They had seen several people like themselves covered in dust and trudging through the precarious obstacle course. Some were still inside cars. Though there weren't many which meant the death toll was likely to be in the high thousands, and if the lack of rescue workers was anything to go by, it meant the devastation extended beyond the borders of the city. She figured there had to have been an evacuation order in place. Maybe after the first quake, only a portion of the city had been hit, maybe communication lines were still working in the north end. It would explain the huge line of bumper-to-bumper traffic. At least it appeared that way. The roads were torn up bad. In all honesty, it was tough to know anything, as that final night was still a blur. Felicity wondered if she was suffering from a mild concussion.

Surely there should have been police, military, rescue workers? It was an unsettling feeling to have more questions than answers. More time passed and by the looks of it, Zeke had given up wandering in circles. One moment he was pressing forward, the next backtracking and circling around areas he'd already passed. There was no clear way through the mess. It reminded Felicity of a maze.

"We'll drive," she muttered staring at Zeke about sixty feet away.

"What?"

Felicity looked over to the other three. "We'll drive to his home."

"Um, I'd like to see that. You got a monster truck? Because that's the only way we are getting through this."

"It can't all be like this. Now I don't know what has

caused this series of earthquakes or even how many there have been since we were in that elevator but not all the roads could have been hit as badly as the city, which means if we can just make it past this, perhaps we can find an abandoned vehicle and use that to get the rest of the way."

Dexter shook his head. "Look around you, Felicity. No cops. No military. No rescue workers, which tells me whatever happened wasn't just some run-of-the-mill earthquake that hit Vegas. Something has happened on a far bigger scale than what we can imagine. Perhaps it was some kind of nuclear weapon or—"

"So you just want to sit here?"

"Where do you expect us to go?"

Ben and Aamir remained quiet, just observing the exchange.

Felicity sighed and was giving more thought to it when her phone dinged, alerting her to the fact it had charged. She pulled off her backpack and slid her finger across the screen and immediately went to her texts. There were twenty-six texts from her father. Most she'd got over the course of the past six months. A couple she hadn't opened, the rest she had clicked on and read the first line and then shut her messaging system down because she was unable to bring herself to read them.

"Anything?" Ben asked.

"I'm checking."

Her eyes scanned through each of them, her heart sinking as she read her father's words, his apologies and then…

"Holy shit."

"What is it?"

"Oh my God."

"Okay, that doesn't sound good. You want to enlighten us?" Dexter asked.

Felicity brought a hand to her mouth as she read the messages. Each one got more desperate the closer it got to the night before the quakes. She swallowed hard as she realized what a fool she'd been. All this time she thought her father had been using scare tactics to get her to return to Florida, but that wasn't the case. She stared at the radar images of the asteroid and scanned through her father's words.

She jumped up and called out to Zeke, time was of the essence.

"Zeke, we're coming with you. We'll find a vehicle once we make it through this mess."

Zeke gave a surprised nod. Dexter scrambled to his feet as Felicity tossed her bag on her back. She wanted to phone her dad again, but the cell wasn't getting any signal. Towers must have collapsed.

"Felicity. Felicity?" Dexter hollered, his voice getting louder. "What is going on?"

She turned her phone around and showed them the radar image of the huge asteroid heading their way.

"What is that?"

"The end of the world."

Chapter 15

It was interesting to see how quickly everyone's tune changed when faced with imminent death. Dexter, who only minutes earlier was protesting about walking, had charged off to get Zeke; Ben, who by any measure should have been the only one complaining because of his leg pain, was now willing to keep pressing on until they found a vehicle; and Aamir, whose mind had been stuck in the past, was now panicking about the future.

Together their minds were whirling. The conversation was filled with positive ideas, anger, and curiosity. Felicity held her phone and read out some of the texts while they picked up the pace and continued heading south. Some of the messages went back as far as six months ago, each of them got more and more urgent.

"Felicity, if you get this message, I need you to come home. Don't discuss this with anyone, just phone me and purchase a plane ticket."

"I haven't heard from you. I'm sorry, Felicity. I don't know what else to say. I've made mistakes. Your father isn't perfect. I care about you and I'm concerned that if you're not back here in Florida, it might be too late."

"Felicity, I know I have acted paranoid in the past but this is not a game. Look at this radar image. This is heading for earth. Now I alerted NASA six months ago and there is a good chance they will make an announcement. Don't wait until that announcement. Once the country hears this, there will be widespread panic. The price of gas will go through the roof. Plane tickets will be hard to get. What I'm trying to say is that now is the time to get back here. I think I can arrange with William some way for us to be part of the list."

"I'm scared for your safety, Felicity. There is a strong possibility that fragments of the asteroid will reach earth long before this mammoth rock will hit. Now I crunched the numbers and ran through data and there appears to be a good chance the smaller meteors will bypass earth but that could change, in which case if that meteor shower hits, there is a strong possibility it will spark worldwide earthquakes,

unlike anything we have ever seen. Either way, you need to get back here now. I can't help you where you are."

They all listened as she read them out. The closer she got to when the first quake happened, the more frequent and desperate her father's texts became.

"And you didn't read these?" Zeke asked.

"I clicked on them but… Look, my relationship with my father hasn't been the best over the years."

Zeke shook his head and instead of blaming her, they focused on the task at hand — that being getting beyond the debris, which would have made it impossible to drive a car.

They took the better part of two hours to reach the city limits. Along the way, they had tried to use phones in several of the stores and hotels in the hope of reaching her father again, but they weren't working. The fact was, the quakes had torn up the ground so badly, power lines, cable lines, anything that was above or below had been torn to shreds. So whether the power grid was down or up throughout the state or country it didn't matter, the devastation had caused so much upheaval, it was practically impossible to communicate. Cell towers would have been the first to collapse. None of them were survival experts, at least that was the impression Felicity got from talking with them. Aamir seemed pretty convinced that the country wasn't experiencing an EMP as that would have wiped out all power, instead, it resulted from a natural disaster — the precursor to a much larger event.

"I still don't get it. What good would there be in bringing you back to Florida if this thing will hit the earth? According to what you've told us about this event that occurred 65 million years ago, it not only would wipe out life on the planet but the earth would be uninhabitable for several years. So unless they have some way of getting off this spinning ball of dirt, we would be screwed."

"My father knows people in government — folks who work for NASA. Chances are if they were alerted to this a year ago, they have been taking steps to instigate a plan of action for the continuity of government."

"And that's why we haven't been alerted," Dexter said. He shook his head, and they continued to head towards a section of road that hadn't been upheaved. It was the first sign of hope they had got since trudging through the city. "You know, I used to watch all these movies about the end of the world. And all the time, they always had this scene in it where the president makes this big announcement. You know, Americans showing a united front and whatnot, in the face of impending doom. But that was all just bull crap. This is true reality. The fact is, the government wouldn't alert everyone."

"Maybe they tried to," Ben said.

"Yeah, and maybe the government doesn't lie." He laughed while shaking his head. "Really, Ben, wake up and smell the coffee. Making an announcement to the country a year ago, or even a few months before the asteroid hits would have created mass panic. We would have seen looting, murder, and violence on a scale larger than we have ever seen. Why? Because no one would have anything to lose. Who's going to put them in jail? Who's going to stop them? No, all those movies were bullshit. The fact is the government officials are doing what they do best — looking after number one." Zeke started laughing again in an almost delirious state. "I knew this day would eventually come. First, my accountant screws me over, then I get fired, then this idiot tries to steal from me, and now the world is going to end? Could it get any worse?"

He kicked a stone thinking it was loose, but it wasn't. He let out a cry and hopped around on one foot while gripping the other. Dexter burst into laughter and slapped him on the back causing him to lose his balance and fall on his ass. "Oh Zekey boy, you really are a hot mess."

Zeke might have got up and tried to throw a punch at him but he was in too much pain. And because everyone continued trudging forward, he whined.

"Oh, that's right. Ben hurts himself and we all rally around and tend to him like Florence Nightingale but I nearly break my foot and you all keep on going. Well go on. See if I care."

No one said a word, they just kept moving forward. They were getting used to his overly dramatic outbursts and attempts at getting attention. A few seconds passed and then they heard him.

"Hold up, guys! Wait up."

Dexter smiled and chuckled under his breath. He loved every minute.

Felicity realized that was something that didn't change in the face of a catastrophic event. People didn't lose their sense of humor. Why would they? They couldn't change anything about what was coming, but they could change how they lived out their last moments.

"Do you think your father could get us out of this?"

"I think my father knows better than anyone what the government is doing to get out of this, and if he wanted me to head home, my guess is yes. He had hope."

"Hope. We could use a little of that right now."

"That and a shot of whiskey," Ben said. "God, I could kill for a glass."

They'd reached a strip of stores where there were numerous vehicles. Some had doors open; most looked like they'd been abandoned in a hurry. Had people got out of vehicles and run into the stores seeking shelter? Whether they were outside or inside, she figured that most people knew in an earthquake to avoid buildings, trees, streetlights and power lines, and to drop, cover and hold. Those in transit were supposed to pull over, stop and stay in their vehicles. But not everyone would have known to do that. Many would have hurried for cover inside buildings, thinking it would have provided some form of safety like getting under a table — except it wouldn't. More people had been killed inside buildings than from falling into crevices.

"Here," Aamir shouted. He ducked into an SUV and turned over the ignition. It rumbled to life, and he beeped the horn before getting out looking triumphant.

"Well done, Ahab," Ben said hopping over. "Well that rules out an EMP, otherwise all the vehicles' computer chips would have been fried. Best guess, the earthquakes have knocked out power lines, and a portion of the country's grid."

They all breathed a sigh of relief as they felt the plush leather interior beneath them. There was something to be said about the familiar and a having a renewed sense of hope. Aamir turned on the radio but nothing came out except static.

"How much gas we got?" Ben asked.

Aamir rubbed a hand over the user interface and wiped away a thin layer of dust. "Three-quarters of a tank. That should get us to Zeke's place."

When Zeke finally made it, he leaned against the door and was panting hard.

"Did you guys not hear me shouting?"

Dexter was lying in the back with his hands clasped behind his head looking all relaxed. "Of course."

Zeke narrowed his gaze and after getting in slammed the door. "All right, Aamir, let's see what kind of driver you are."

"Buckle up. This might be bumpy," he said adjusting

his mirrors and spraying washer fluid over the windshield. Up front, Ben rooted through the glove compartment. He tossed out a bunch of receipts, a vehicle manual and then pulled out a handgun.

"You feeling lucky, punk?" he joked while rolling it back and forth between his two hands.

"Is it loaded?" Felicity asked. Ben dropped out the magazine.

"Seems so."

"Let me see that," Dexter said leaning forward.

Zeke was quick to respond. "Do not give it to him. He's liable to shoot us in the back and leave us for dead."

"Oh shut up." He kept his hand out and Ben handed it over. "Desert Eagle .50 caliber. Nice." Dexter turned to Zeke and he went quiet for a second before Dexter laughed and handed it back to Ben.

"Well, let's get this shit show on the road, I say we forget heading to Zeke's and try to see how close we can get to Florida."

"Florida?" Zeke muttered as Aamir reversed back and

pulled out of the lot. "Forget Florida, I'm going home. Why the hell would I travel to Florida?"

"To live? Uh, wake up. Didn't anything about what she said sink in? There is an asteroid that will wipe out life as we know it."

"So?"

Felicity's eyebrows shot up. "You don't want to survive?"

"All I have been doing is surviving, Felicity. For the past ten years."

"Oh here we go, sob story of the month," Dexter said tapping his fingers against the door as Aamir zigzagged around traffic and mounds of debris. He turned down several streets to avoid crevices and rubble, and mostly stayed on Valley View Boulevard until they got to the outskirts of town.

It was a mess everywhere they turned. Fires burning, houses collapsed, vehicles overturned, massive sections of road upheaved and crevices that fissured across the landscape like a cracked windshield. At no point along the way did they see rescue crews, police or FEMA.

It was just pure darkness, mixed with fire.

"Feels like we are in hell itself," Ben muttered.

There were others out there. They saw them, the silhouettes of people milling around vehicles, some had started them and had the same idea to get out of the city. The farther they got from the main city the more people they saw, which led them to believe that in the first twenty-four hours after the earthquake hit, residents had evacuated the city. Some had escaped while others had perished. After two earthquakes, they figured there had to have been more, and that was the reason emergency services weren't anywhere to be found. They had probably gone out to do their job but ended up suffering the same fate as others.

Felicity shook her head in disbelief. So many lives had been lost.

The journey to Henderson was slow, and took longer than they expected but that was because as darkness fell it became harder to see what sections of road were cracked.

Aamir flipped on the high beams and did his best to navigate the maze. Though it wasn't as bad as the city, it was still treacherous and one wrong turn could have meant certain death.

It didn't help that they could still feel tremors every so often, leading them to believe another quake was imminent. At some point along the way, everyone except Aamir, Felicity and Zeke fell asleep. Exhaustion was at an all-time high. Perhaps it was the gentle rumble of the vehicle, or that this was the first time since exiting the Luxor that they'd been able to rest.

Felicity cut Zeke a glance.

"You mentioned you have kids, Zeke?"

He tossed her a stare from inside the darkened vehicle. "Three."

"What ages?"

"Four, twelve and nineteen."

"They live in Vegas?"

"Nope. One is in Australia, another in New York and one in Tampa."

"Why so widespread?"

"I met their mothers while I was on tour."

She nodded. "Groupies?"

"I didn't say that."

"Then what?"

He shrugged and seem hesitant to open up. She was keen to understand why he didn't want to go to Florida. He had given up for the most part. While she couldn't be certain if her father had a means of saving her, she wasn't just going to give up.

"Look, I'd rather not talk about it. I just want to get home."

"Sure," she nodded, casting a gaze outside. Unlike the others, he was a bit of a closed book. He seemed to live his life from a distance. Probably because that's all he'd known. As they made their way into a sprawling estate in Henderson, Zeke perked up.

"We're getting close," he said out loud, waking the other two. He leaned forward and gave directions to Aamir. From the little they could see under the wash of the headlights, many of the expensive homes that once attracted the wealthy were now lying in ruins.

The nearer they got, the more excited Zeke became.

"I've got a generator there, so we should be good for a while if you want to stay the night."

"Stay the night? What planet are you living on?" Dexter blurted out as he rubbed his tired eyes. "We are dropping your ass off and getting the hell out of here."

Zeke ignored him and kept rattling off what he would do: take a shower, have his chef cook him a meal, sleep in his own bed. He was living a fantasy, his mind was still stuck in the past. That all changed when they pulled into the long driveway that led up to his mountaintop mansion. Though it was still intact, it wasn't empty.

Aamir slammed the brakes on.

"Friends of yours?" he asked.

Zeke leaned forward, and they all took in the sight of multiple motorbikes, a gathering of what looked to be a motorcycle gang.

Chapter 16

Zeke sat there contemplating what to do. He hadn't banked on this. This wasn't supposed to be happening. As he looked at the four motorcycles parked out front, and the light emanating from his home, his thoughts went to the Desert Eagle in the glove compartment.

For over twenty-four hours he'd been in hell and he was in no mood to deal with a bunch of greasy ass bikers, even if they could probably snap his spine.

"Well, that's that. Let's go," Dexter said tapping Aamir on the arm.

Before he shifted the gearstick into reverse, Zeke pushed out and slid around to the passenger door. He yanked it open and Dexter looked up at him. Instantly he went for the glove compartment but before he could get it open, Dexter slammed his foot against it.

"Are you out of your mind? Do you want to die?"

He looked back at his home. "That's my house and

I've had about as much as I can take for one day."

"What? So you plan on going all Dirty Harry on them?"

"Just move your leg, Dexter."

"Get back in, Zeke, we are getting out of here."

"I'm not going anywhere."

"Then you're not taking the gun. That's the only one we have and God willing we won't have to use it but if we do, I'm not wasting bullets on a group of bikers who will be dead soon, anyway."

Zeke stared at him. He shook his head. It wasn't like he was stupid. He'd heard them talking about an asteroid heading towards earth but the reality of the end hadn't sunk in. Hell, he still hadn't come to grips with his career being over.

"Move your leg," he repeated through gritted teeth.

"No."

"Fine, then I'll deal with this my way."

Zeke slammed the door and marched away, scooping up a twisted-off metal pole laying in the street. While the estate homes hadn't fared well, he could see why these assholes had moved in on his house. It was one of four that hadn't been reduced to a pile of rubble. It had suffered damage, the walls were cracked and a portion of the west wing had collapsed but beyond that it was still standing. That was a testament to the quality. He'd spent twenty-seven million to get the property created, not that he'd used it much. As the attendance on his evening shows had waned, he'd asked Jerry to convince the Luxor managers to let him hold an afternoon show. That way they could draw in some of the visitors who didn't want to take in the evening show. For a while, it worked. Numbers went back up and his management and the Luxor were happy again. That all ended when his constant use of prescription drugs finally got the better of him.

Zeke heard Dexter call out to him but he ignored him and continued to press on towards the home. Bikers or not, there was no way in hell anyone would rob him of the last few pleasures of existence before his life came to an end. As he squeezed the metal pipe in his hand, he saw Jerry's face, then the new kid who'd taken his career. Rage welled up in him.

As he passed the Harleys out front, he had a good mind to go nuclear on them but he had a better idea. The closer he got to his home he saw them through the windows, helping themselves to his wine, from his vintage wine cellar that was worth thousands of dollars. He'd had it created for the basement and had even worked out an agreement with a wine estate in California to send him cases of wine every month.

Drink my wine? Help yourself to my food? He thought.

He was within spitting distance of the door when Dexter came up beside him and grabbed him.

"Use your common sense, Zeke. There are four of them."

"And?"

"They are probably armed."

"So give me the gun."

"It doesn't matter," Felicity added as she hurried up to join them. "None of this does. You're so concerned about what they are taking from you but if we don't shift our ass and get on the road, you aren't going to be here to enjoy it."

"Who said I want to live?"

Dexter snorted. "I told you. This guy is crazy. I'm done!" he said wiping his hands as he walked away. Felicity still had a hold of Zeke's jacket as he was eyeing the side entrance.

"What is it, Zeke? What has happened to you that you would care so little for your own life?"

He was breathing in hard and grinding his teeth.

"So you lost your job. Big deal. People lose their job every day in America. At least you had a career. Few people will ever get to know what that was like. To have a TV show, travel the world and have hundreds of people paying good money to see you perform five days a week." She pointed back to the car. "Aamir has busted his ass for twelve hours a day, seven days a week for years for little thanks. Dexter has been living on the streets, having to steal to pay for his next meal. Ben, well… he was one hair away from having loan sharks end his life, and I don't even need to explain my life." She studied him. "You want to go in there and fight over possessions which will be gone in who knows, seventy-two hours, then go ahead but by the looks of those men, you aren't even going to last that." She released her grip and placed a hand on her hip and looked off towards the car. "Now I don't know if my father has a plan to get us out of this impending mess or if any of us will survive but I know this. If these are the last hours I have left on this planet, I don't want to spend them alone. I've spent the last two years of my life alone, keeping those I love at a distance for ridiculous reasons. All so I wouldn't get hurt, all because I allowed my pride to get the better of me. Now, all I want to do is get to Florida, see my father. I hope he's still alive."

"And if he's not?"

"Then. Well," she shrugged. "At least I didn't spend the final hours of my life alone."

Zeke looked back at the car where the other three were waiting patiently. He sighed.

"Look, you said you had a kid in Tampa. Maybe he's still alive. Wouldn't you want to see him before the end?"

"His mother and I…"

"Don't get along? Join the club. Who the hell gets along in today's world?"

Zeke looked back through the window. He could hear the bikers inside laughing up a storm, smashing his property and causing general mayhem. Slowly he nodded and turned to walk back towards the car. "Okay."

Felicity placed a hand on his back and they walked back down the driveway when the door to the house opened.

"I thought I heard someone out here. Hey, boys, you said you wanted pussy, it looks like the good lord delivered."

Zeke closed his eyes tight, ground his teeth and went to turn but Felicity shook her head and tugged him towards the vehicle.

"Oh, hey, don't go. The party has just started, come on back."

Zeke cast a glance over his shoulder and saw two other guys stumble out, bottles in their hands. One was a bottle of his Chateau Margaux. That cost him $225,000. In that instant, he saw red. Zeke turned back getting a good grip on the steel pole and slapping it against his hand.

"That wine is mine."

"And a fine wine it is."

"Put it down."

The bikers laughed. "Is this fucking guy for real?"

One more biker came out chuckling to himself, then his eyes locked onto Zeke.

"Well shit me if it isn't Zeke Blackstone himself. Holy crap. The man in person."

"Zeke, don't."

Zeke had stopped listening to Felicity's words the second they stepped outside.

Laughter soon dissipated when they caught sight of him slapping the steel bar against his hand.

"Are you for real?" one of them said.

"Get the fuck out of my place."

They stared back at him blankly and then burst out laughing and mocked him. "Get the fuck out of my place," one said in the most condescending tone. "Really? How about you make us!"

The one holding the expensive bottle of wine released it and it smashed on the ground. Zeke's gaze dropped to the ground and then he lifted the bar. "I'm gonna…"

"You're gonna what?" One of them pulled a Glock from his waistband. "Huh? What you gonna do? Ricky, bring that sweet bit of ass over here."

"Don't touch her!" Zeke said stepping between Felicity and Ricky.

The guy who was holding the gun lunged forward and placed the piece against the side of his face. "Rethink what you are about to do. I know what you're thinking. You're thinking, I could be the hero. But to that I say… don't." He grinned. "Now put the bar down and get inside."

Ricky grabbed a hold of Felicity and she kneed him in the nuts. "Get the hell off me."

They heard a car door open and the biker holding the gun turned his attention towards the car. Foolish or not that was all he needed. Zeke threw a right hook and caught him on the face. Now they might have got the better of them but the other two greasy assed bikers stepped in and took him down and pummeled him.

"Get off him!" Felicity yelled as she was being dragged inside. The guy Zeke just hit told them to get the others in the car. However, before they could do anything, Dexter jumped back in the vehicle and Aamir backed out at a fast rate of speed.

The main guy let out a laugh.

"Look at that motor go. Well, say goodbye to your friends."

Struggling, spitting and yelling, Zeke continued to curse them while trying to get free.

* * *

Felicity was thrown to the ground and kicked in the

back several times to get her to be compliant. She let out a cry and tears welled up in her eyes.

"Tito, don't bruise up the lady."

"Bitch won't stop struggling."

Zeke put up one hell of a fight. They continued to beat him into submission even as he lay on the floor and was no longer fighting back.

"Leave him alone!" she screamed. "He's not even fighting back."

"Not now he isn't," the main guy said waving around the gun. He came over and grabbed a hold of Felicity by the face, squeezing her cheeks together. He had a thick straggly beard and long slick hair swept back over his head. His breath smelled of alcohol and cigarettes, and he reeked like hadn't washed in a week. All of them were wearing leather and had a patch on the back of a Grim Reaper and the name: Brothers of Mayhem. "Now how about we get acquainted. What's your name, darlin'?"

Felicity pursed her lips refusing to speak.

"Come on now, cat got your tongue?" He smiled. "I'm

Mac, that's Ricky, Doc and Tito, and you are?"

She spat in his face. He jerked back and then wiped a hand across his face before licking it. "Oh, I think I'm gonna like you." Without a moment's hesitation, he backhanded her. A shot of pain went through her. It stung so bad. For half a second the world went black.

"Well boys, let's bring our guests into the living room. Now I'm thinking a rich asshole like Blackstone has to have a stash of coke around here somewhere. So… where is it, Zeke?"

Out the corner of her eye, she could see Zeke on the floor squirming around and groaning.

"Get him up."

They grabbed a hold of him and hauled him to his feet and he winced, holding his rib cage.

"The coke? Where?"

"Screw you."

"Wrong answer," Doc said throwing a gut punch. This continued for another minute until Mac intervened and got down real close to his face and asked him again.

"If you don't tell me, I will be forced to put a bullet in this girls head. So… let's try this again."

Zeke cast a glance over to Felicity.

This time he avoided another harsh beating.

Zeke told him to go into the bedroom and look in the closet. It was stored inside a shoe box.

* * *

Aamir drove backward out of the lot, spun the vehicle around and floored it.

"Where the hell are you going?" Ben said leaning forward. "Go back."

"Screw that, keep going, Aamir. I warned him. I knew he would fuck everything up. But oh no, he wouldn't listen. Mr. Big Shot had to play the hero, well now he can lie in the bed he's made."

"Felicity is back there."

Dexter gave a nod. "Unfortunate, but shit happens."

"Shit happens?" Ben yelled. He tapped Aamir on the shoulder. "Turn around now and head back."

Aamir slammed his foot on the brake and all of them

shot forward in their seats.

"Aamir, unless you want to end up dead, don't listen to him."

"Turn the vehicle around," Ben hollered again, scowling at Dexter.

Aamir went to do it but Dexter stopped him from shifting the gear. Back and forth they argued until he couldn't take it anymore. Aamir shut off the engine and got out of the car taking the keys with him.

"What the hell are you doing?" Dexter said, pushing out and tossing his hands up.

"Stop shouting. Both of you! You are confusing me."

"Look, this is straightforward, we go back, we die. We leave, we live. What part of that is confusing?"

Ben got out of the vehicle and hobbled over to him. "Don't listen to him. We need to head back. We are not leaving her there. This isn't about Zeke. If we leave her back there, you know what they will do."

Aamir stared at him.

Ben stepped forward and put his hand out. "If you

don't want to go back, just give me the keys and I'll go myself."

Dexter leaned against the car and shook his head before making his way around to the driver's side.

"Am I the only one here with common sense? You want to put our lives in danger for two people we don't even know?"

Ben turned and jabbed a finger into his chest.

"Look around you. How many people have you seen on the streets? We might be the only ones alive. Now there is a big ass asteroid heading towards this planet. I don't know how long we have got but I know that the only chance we have of surviving it, is Felicity. So I'm going back. If you want to stay here, stay but just remember who saved your ass back in Vegas."

"That was a joint effort."

"Exactly!" Ben tore the keys out of Aamir's hands and trudged back to the car.

Chapter 17

The Sikorsky UH-60 Black Hawk swept low over Vegas as it came in for a landing. Charlie peered out of the side taking in the devastation. The journey had taken them the better part of four hours. He'd seen nothing like it. The devastation across the United States from the precursor to the asteroid's arrival was huge. Multiple impacts from small meteors had seriously pissed off Mother Nature.

The last time an event of this magnitude occurred was over 780,000 years ago.

His mind drifted back to one of his lectures.

"From what we know, geologists were able to see what occurred by gathering tektites."

"Sir, what is that?"

"It's a natural glass which is commonly found in meteor and asteroid debris. Anyway, they discovered this in Asia,

Australia, Canada and Central America and based on their findings they could determine that the earth was hit approximately at the same time in different spots. Now it's widely accepted that this occurred roughly 793,000 years ago. The interesting part is that the tektites that were found in Central America were very different in composition to those found elsewhere which meant there were separate impacts. However, what all of them have in common is the period of time. The Central American impacts occurred at the same time as the Australian."

"So what was the devastation?"

He turned and faced the class.

"Fires, earthquakes, and tsunamis 100 meters high. There would have also been dust and gas tossed up into the atmosphere which would have blocked the sunlight and lowered the temperature."

"Doctor Meyer, keep back from the door. We are coming in for a landing," Lieutenant Tom Harley said, snapping Charlie back into the present moment. The devastation of the meteor impacts hadn't been as bad as it was 793,000 years ago. While William was right, they had made a mistake in their calculations and while some of the meteors had hit the earth, not all of it had. If it had, they would have been in a far worse situation than this.

"Pretty bad, eh?" Harley said.

"Not as bad as it could have been."

He chuckled. "You science guys are crazy. All I see is a disaster, and all you see is data. But you know what? I don't care as long as we get your daughter and get home. You must know people in high places to have managed to pull off this order."

Charlie glanced at him but said nothing, his mind was a highway full of traffic. He was worried about his daughter, feeling guilty about the loss of life that would occur and fearful about the future. The longest anyone had spent in space was eight hundred and sixty-eight days, approximately twenty-eight months. If they got off this planet before the asteroid hit, they were looking at being up there for at least two years. Now as far as he knew, NASA hadn't the technology to allow for that but William seemed confident.

Harley looked as if the pilot was saying something to him over his earpiece as he would do this thing with his head, where he would turn it to the side and frown. The noise of the rotors was deafening. He'd been on several planes in his life but no helicopters. He hated flying at the best of times so this was definitely one for the books.

"Doctor Meyer, the pilot is going to try and bring it down over there," he pointed to a clearing. Charlie nodded. It was really bad on the ground. Huge areas of the road had been flipped over like an omelet, revealing the guts of the earth beneath it. Signposts were twisted and snapped off, vehicles swallowed up. Everywhere his eyes scanned there was nothing but gray dust covering every inch of the ground. The buildings that had survived stood out like sore thumbs. They looked out of place, abnormal among an ocean of debris and ruins.

They'd seen several survivors, not everyone was dead.

"Now we can't be down there long. There is a going to

be a lot of desperate people thinking we are the cavalry. I won't have this Black Hawk compromised."

"I highly doubt anyone will fly off in it, lieutenant," Charlie said before looking back out as they got closer to the ground. "They will be lucky to even get near us."

"Either way, we get in, find your daughter and get out. If she's not there, my orders are to leave immediately. No ifs or buts, do you understand?"

Charlie nodded.

Harley gazed out and shook his head. "Even if that asteroid wasn't coming, I couldn't see us coming back from this. This is nuts."

The pilot brought down the Hawk, and the rotors thumped hard, kicking up a plume of dust. Back in Cape Canaveral, Charlie had been told to put on some combat gear. At first, he balked at the idea but after getting the rundown from Harley on what they'd experienced evacuating government officials, he agreed. Not everyone had taken a liking to seeing military choppers flying overhead, landing, gathering a few people and leaving the rest.

The unrest in the country was bad enough before the shit hit the fan but now, well, tempers would flare and some people would take matters into their own hands while the rest would look on in shock, wondering why their government had abandoned them.

It was to be expected.

As the pilot set the Black Hawk down, the thump, thump of the rotors was the only sound that could be heard. The pilot turned around. "Thirty minutes and then we are gone."

Harley tossed up a thumb.

"Okay! Let's move out," Harley said hopping out and running at a crouch away from the helicopter. Charlie followed in his shadow until they were clear. It would take a few minutes to reach the Mirage. The helicopter had landed about half a mile from it.

"Lieutenant, you got any family?"

"Wife and two kids. A boy that is six and a girl that is nine."

"They back at the base?"

He gave a nod but didn't look at him. He was all business. Charlie had met several military guys over his years working with William. Most of them were decent guys, some had a killer sense of humor, but then there were the quiet ones that once they put that uniform on, they were all business. Harley struck him as that kind of guy.

"What if they weren't?"

The LT glanced at him as if he had told a joke and he didn't find it funny.

"I'm just saying I appreciate what you are doing."

"I'm doing my job. I didn't pick this assignment. If I had my way, you would still be back at the base."

"I'm just saying…"

"Well don't. I should be alongside my brothers helping them instead we're here offering special treatment to someone who…"

"… alerted the United States to an oncoming asteroid," Charlie said, cutting him off.

Harley frowned. "I thought that was our NASA guys."

"Yeah, contrary to what most people think, NASA doesn't spot everything."

He nodded and looked off into the distance.

"So we have you to thank?"

"I wouldn't say that because had the government actually done its job, there might have been a lot more people they could have saved."

"Only so many people can fit on the *Deliverance*. Resources will be maxed out with those that are going. Unfortunately, you can't save everyone, doc. Trust me. I've done four tours over in Iraq and there are many times we have had to fly away and leave behind people we knew would get slaughtered, bombed or suffer some terrible fate. It's just the way it is."

Charlie didn't reply. He knew he was right, but that didn't make it any easier.

They trudged on working their way around debris and jogging when they could. It felt like they were in a concrete jungle that had been plowed. He coughed several times trying to clear his throat. The air was thick with dust.

As they made it into the hotel lobby, Charlie was the first one in the door. His eyes flitted from side to side and he called out her name. “Felicity! Felicity.”

There was no answer.

Harley raked his M4 around the room and stood near the entranceway looking out for anyone that might have seen them heading in. Charlie hurried through the hotel calling out her name and searching as many rooms as he could. Some areas were impossible to reach. The longer he was in there, the more his stomach sank.

It was his worst fear.

Where have you gone?

Charlie leaned against a wall and slumped down onto the floor. He gripped at some of the debris and closed his eyes. He didn’t want to head back to the lobby because he knew what Harley would say and he couldn’t bring himself to leave — not without her.

On the floor, he reached into his pocket and pulled

out his wallet, from that he fished out a photo of his wife, him and Felicity back when she was only ten.

He'd been such a foolish man.

Losing his wife to cancer might have put him inside a mental ward if it wasn't for his work. As clichéd as it might have seemed, throwing himself into his work kept him sane throughout it all. The first time Kathy had got cancer he was there by her side, going with her to all the doctors' meetings and standing with her through therapy.

She'd always said if it came back, and it was final, she didn't want him to be there but he knew that wasn't true. Their entire marriage she had always supported him through every endeavor. His work had allowed her to be at home with Felicity. That was both a blessing and a curse because it meant Felicity saw Kathy as being there and saw him as always being absent but that wasn't the case. He did it so she could be there for their daughter. Few mothers today got the chance to be there for their kids as they grew up. No matter what she told Felicity, he never fully understood that so it wasn't a surprise when she got angry over the way he acted when the cancer came back. He couldn't deal with it. A life without his wife just didn't seem real. It was unfair. Why? He had raged against God and prayed that he would take him instead of her. Why her? Why then?

"Charlie!" Harley's voice came from his left.

He looked up to see him standing nearby, his rifle down low.

"Any luck?"

He shook his head.

"Then we need to go."

"Just leave me here. You head out. I will find my daughter."

"I can't do that. My orders were to bring you here and then get you back."

"Lieutenant. I'm not leaving my daughter out there."

He crouched down beside Charlie and placed a hand on his shoulder. "I know this is hard but you've seen it out there. Trying to find her would be like searching for a needle in a haystack. We don't have the fuel to do flyovers. Now the pilot is waiting for us otherwise he will take off. He has his own orders and I am not dying out here."

"Because you have a family to get back to, right?" Charlie said looking up at him.

Harley sighed. He got on the radio to the pilot.

"We are on our way back."

He released the button on the side of it and stared at Charlie before grabbing a hold of him and hauling him up. "Let's go."

Reluctantly he pressed on until they made their way out of the hotel. Outside he called out her name again, one last time. "Felicity!"

He waited, desperately hoping for a response but got nothing.

Harley broke into a jog and he followed him. As they came up around a corner, there were two survivors rooting through a car. As soon as the two guys saw them, their eyes widened.

"I knew it. I knew you guys would come."

A black guy came racing over. Part of his face was covered in blood. The other one had his arm in a makeshift sling. "Where's the rest of you?"

"Back away," Harley barked out.

"What?"

"You heard me."

Charlie tried to intervene as he had a feeling what was about to happen if he didn't.

The black guy looked confused. He peered past them, no doubt assuming they were part of a larger group. "Where are the others?"

"There are no others."

"Then how did you get here?"

"Sir, I will not tell you again. Back up."

"We just need some water."

There was water on the helicopter. Charlie walked up to where Harley was and spoke into his ear. "Out of the question," Harley replied.

"You want them to die out here?"

"My orders were clear."

"Bend them."

"No. Now back up."

"Oh, I see. I see how it is," the man said backing up as Harley raised the M4 at him. Just off in the distance, three more people stumbled over mounds of debris.

"Doc, we need to go, now move it."

"Lieutenant."

"I won't say it again. Move your ass."

Charlie gritted his teeth and slipped around him while Harley kept the rifle trained on the two survivors. They broke away and jogged through the maze making their way back to the helicopter. When they arrived, the pilot was out of the bird and holding up an assault rifle to keep back four more survivors trying to approach.

Harley fired off a few warning rounds. "Get back!"

These survivors didn't look threatening. They appeared confused, and rightly so.

"Where the hell have you two been?" the pilot yelled.

"Ask him," Harley muttered as they hurried over and got into the Black Hawk. Harley kept his gun trained on a cluster of them as more came into view. The survivors must have thought they were the beginnings of help to come. But no one was coming. The government would leave them to perish with the rest of the world. For them, it was just a matter of time and it would be all over.

The rotors thumped out, sending out a wash of air and dust.

As the Hawk lifted off the ground, Charlie tossed out a few bottles of water.

"What the hell are you doing?"

He looked back at him. "Showing a little compassion. Maybe you should try it sometime."

Chapter 18

They sat on the floor, side by side, watching the bikers indulge in the large bag of coke.

"Oh, this is good shit. Man, you rich assholes really know how to get your hands on the pure stuff. You remember that bad batch we had down in Florida that time?" Mac said to Tito. "I still have nightmares over that. But, God damn, this is magic."

He sniffed hard and wiped away the dust from the bottom of his nose. He grinned at both of them as his buddies waited for their turn. Mac walked over and crouched down in front of them and offered them a swig of his beer.

"You want some?"

Felicity shook her head.

"Come on. You're looking at me like I'm the big bad wolf. I'm not the enemy here."

"No, you're the thief," Zeke said.

He laughed at Zeke and got up and pulled out a pack of smokes. "You need to be careful what you say, Blackstone. I've killed people for saying less than that." He lit his cigarette and pulled up a chair before spinning it around and taking a seat.

His eyes drifted around the room. "Must be nice having so much money you can own a place like this."

"It's called hard work. But I'm sure that's foreign to you."

"I'll have you know me and the guys here know a lot about business, don't we, guys?" he said shouting over his shoulder. They grunted and Tito nodded. "Yeah, before all of this shit storm we were just like you. Weaving our magic and creating custom bikes." He paused and blew smoke into Zeke's face. "But that's right, you see the patch on our back, you see the way we dress and you immediately think we are some rogue gang that roamed the country doing home invasions. Don't you?"

Zeke shrugged. "I don't give a shit."

"But you would be wrong. Tito, how much money did

we bring in last year?"

"Just shy of a million dollars."

"Okay, it wasn't on the level of what you were probably raking in but we were contributing taxpayers. Yep, business owners offering a service. In fact, that's what brought us to your neck of the woods. You see, we had a client out here that was expecting delivery of their new custom bike when those meteors hit."

"Meteors?" Felicity piped up.

"Oh, found your tongue," he said before laughing.

"Screw you."

"Darlin', I might just take you up on that offer." He sniffed hard and took another swig of his drink. "But getting back to your question. Yeah, fucking multiple rocks came out of nowhere. We took cover inside a house just two streets down from this. Not that it would help. Sure, the house wasn't leveled by falling rock but the earthquakes that followed soon dealt with that. Anyway, after we crawled out from our hellhole, we were going to head back to Vegas but before all this happened, our client had told us that good old Blackstone lived nearby. Yeah, he was raving about how you had this top-of-the-line house, multiple sports cars and that you were a real narcissistic asshole. Now had this shit storm not happened, we might have just driven by your place out of curiosity, you know, seen where you lived and observed from afar like most do. But after what happened, we figured we'd pay you a visit, especially being as your home was one of the few that stayed upright. Sure, the west side is fucked up but you must have spent some coin on this place to make sure it could handle a quake."

Zeke remained quiet and didn't take his eyes off Mac. Felicity thought if he wasn't tied and there was only him, and Mac, he would have torn him limb from limb.

"Blackstone, you better wipe that frown off your face real quick. I could have had one of the boys shoot you but I haven't. In fact, we have done nothing but treat you decent."

"Decent?" That was it. Felicity couldn't contain herself. "You've beaten us multiple times since we've been here. You call that decent?"

"Darlin', what did you expect me to do? Let you two lunatics go berserk?"

"You do know the police will show up here? They are already out there. We saw them on the way in. Yep, it won't be long before they come knocking to make sure Zeke here is okay, and then you are all screwed."

He took another swig and laughed. "I like you. Really. Damn. You're a good-looking woman. Let me guess." His eyes darted to Zeke. "You're his girlfriend, right? Oh, no, wait. He picked you up on the Strip, seventy bucks for a blow, is that the going rate now, Tito?" he said turning around to get an answer.

"Something like that."

"But you didn't hire her for that, did you, Zeke? You probably convinced her to come back for the whole night with your buddies. Which reminds me, where do you think your buddies have gone?"

Felicity just scowled at him. There was no point trying to clarify or defend herself. The guy was an animal. Doc went over to the window and looked out.

"They out there?"

He shook his head.

"Oh dear, looks like your buddies abandoned you. You should really think about getting some new friends." He chuckled as he got up from his chair. He cast one more glance at them before asking them if they wanted a beer. When they didn't respond he went into the kitchen to get himself another. While he did that, Felicity moved her hands behind her back trying to get out of the restraints. All they'd used was some cloth as they couldn't find any rope.

"What are you doing?" Zeke said in a low voice.

"What do you think?" she replied, just as she managed to pry loose one of her hands. Right after, he returned and twisted the lid off the bottle.

"I've got to say, Zeke, you've got a nice setup here. The backup generator, all the food, and drink in your basement and kitchen. I think we will be doing just fine while we wait for society to pick up the pieces."

"Or the cops come and put your ass in jail."

"Darlin', nice try but we aren't stupid. No one is coming. In fact, we were surprised to see you. We've seen the roads and damage out there. Even if the cops are still in operation, they will have their hands full for the next two years dealing with clean-up. Trust me. No one is coming. So sit back and relax. I have a few ideas for what we can do to pass the time."

He took a long hard pull on the beer and eyed her, his eyes scanning up and down her body.

* * *

Ben parked the car just beyond the mouth of the road that led up to Zeke's property. He'd kept the headlights turned off and made sure it was out of view before he got out holding the gun low.

"Ben, wait. What the hell are you planning to do? Just go in there shooting?"

"If I have to."

"No, we need to think about this. Develop a plan of action. Think about how we can escape if things get a little hot."

"You mean, how you will escape?"

Dexter put up a finger. "I'm just trying to be safe here. I think you and Aamir would agree that we don't want to end up with a bullet in us. So if we are going to do this, we need to do it right."

"And what's your plan?" Ben asked checking the magazine before keeping an eye on the house from the corner of a home that had been destroyed, except for one wall.

"I don't have a plan. I'm just saying… we need to go slow..."

Ben ignored him and hurried out, his leg throbbing as he broke into a hobbled jog.

"… or we can go fast," Dexter added, trying to keep up with them.

With no streetlights, their movements were unseen. Three figures darted along the street and made their way to the side of the house. When they made it, Ben pressed his back against the wall and shuffled along to a window.

He peered in and caught sight of one man. He ducked down and made a gesture with his hand to show that there was one. At a crouch, he moved on to the next window and peered over. He couldn't see anyone in there and was about to move away when another one guy appeared. This one headed over to the window. Ben ducked, and he heard him open it.

That's when the voices seeped out.

"Hey! Shut that."

"C'mon man, I need fresh air."

"Shut the window," a voice yelled. "You're letting in all the dust."

The guy muttered to himself as he closed it. All the while all three of them were crouched down low. "Ben. Think about this. For their sake, we need to be careful."

"And we will." He continued on until they came around the back. There were French doors covered up by blinds. As he neared them he heard someone approaching. He turned and waved them back to the corner of the house. The door opened and someone stepped out.

"I'm having a smoke," the guy hollered.

It was the same guy who'd wanted to open the window. They watched him for a minute or two as he lit a cigarette and then wandered over to the swimming pool, unzipped and took a piss in it. He was mumbling some tune to himself and banging his head while looking around. Dexter shook his head and mouthed the word. "No."

"Yes," Ben said, slipping off his shoes and moving quickly towards the man. His ankle still hurt badly, but he pushed the pain from his mind to focus on the task at hand. His mind was going in circles, and his pulse racing as he hurried over and came up behind the guy. Ben pressed the gun against the back of his neck.

"Make one fucking sound and I'll end you. Now turn to your right and walk."

The guy put up his hands and spat his cigarette out. "You are so fucked."

"Yeah, maybe, but I'm not the one who has a gun at

the back of my head right now."

Dexter had been keeping an eye on the door while Ben guided the beefy-looking biker over to the corner of the house.

"How many more of you inside?"

"Fuck you."

Ben pistol-whipped him across the back of the head and he collapsed. "Now, let's try that again. How many?"

"There's just the four of us."

"Aamir, check him over."

Aamir rooted through his pockets and then patted him down until he found a revolver in the back of his waistband. "Nice. We'll take that."

Ben grabbed a hold of him by the back of the neck. "Get up!" He turned and motioned for Dexter, and they slowly backed away from the house until they were at a safe distance. Once they were out of sight, he had Dexter and Aamir keep an eye on him while he went to the corner of the house and waited. It would only be a matter of time before they clued in.

As he waited at the corner his mind flashed back to the day everything went wrong.

"You want to borrow $50,000?"

"You know I'm good for it."

"You paid up because we tracked you down."

"But I paid."

Ben had dealt with loan sharks before. His numerous trips on business took him to Las Vegas twice a month, each time it was the same, he would get business out of the way and then he would hit the casinos. Sometimes he scored big, but more often than not he would walk out with empty pockets. After a string of bad luck, he'd realized that he'd spent everything he had. That's when he came across a loan shark who offered loans at crazy interest rates. The first few times he used them it went well. He never borrowed too much and always cut his losses if he got close to losing the money he owed. Only on two occasions had he gone over the amount, but he eventually paid them back. The night before the earthquake, he'd borrowed $50,000. It was way more than he'd ever taken and he knew if he fucked up, they weren't going to just beat the shit out of him, his life would be over. He'd heard the horror stories of them tossing people off buildings, cutting their fingers off and taking them out into the Nevada desert and burying them alive. He just figured it wouldn't happen to him. He was wrong. That night he lost everything. When he stepped into that elevator he was planning on going up to the top floor and committing suicide. If he was going out, he was going out on his own terms. But it seemed fate had another idea.

"Tito!" a voice bellowed snapping him back into the moment. "Where the hell are you?"

He cast a glance back at the biker who was on his knees with his hands behind his head. Aamir had the gun near the back of his head.

"I'm afraid your pal is a little busy," Ben hollered out.

The biker heard him as his eyes darted around and he

backed away, disappearing inside the house. A minute or two passed and Zeke emerged with one biker behind him. He pushed him out holding a gun to his head. They shouted out into the darkness.

"Now unless you want your buddy's brains all over the driveway, release him now!"

"No can do," Ben shouted. "And if you put a bullet in him, I will cut every finger off Tito's hands, and believe me, that's gonna hurt like a bitch!"

There was a moment's hesitation. He had no idea if the guy would shoot Zeke but he figured that if they were smart, they would head back in and think things over. Sure enough, that's what he did. A few minutes passed, and they retreated inside.

"So?" Dexter asked getting near.

"Now we wait."

"Wait? That's your big plan?"

"Hell, none of this was my plan. I was thinking we would use you as a distraction while I slipped in and got them out but fate gave me a better idea."

"Fate?"

"Yeah, the thing that saved our lives, and if it's in the cards, will save theirs."

Chapter 19

Twenty minutes passed and still there was no sign of them.

"What the hell do you think they are doing?" Aamir asked. Ben was getting antsy. It was dark out and there was a possibility they could have slipped out the back and were making their way around. He kept scanning the surrounding perimeter for figures lurking in the dark. If the bikers were out there, they could kill them before they even returned fire.

"Ben. We need to do something," Dexter said.

"I've got an idea but you're not going to like it."

"Listen, if it means we don't have to stand out here all night, I'm all ears."

He was just about to share it with him when Tito chuckled to himself.

"What so funny?" Dexter asked.

"You guys are so fucked. If you'd been smart, you

would have stayed away."

"Well, maybe we aren't smart. Or maybe we like killing people to let off frustration."

He continued to laugh. At first, Dexter ignored it but then he couldn't handle it anymore. Before Ben could stop him, he rushed over to the guy and pistol-whipped him across the face causing him to topple over. "Now shut the fuck up!"

Dexter walked back and Ben stared at him.

"What?"

"Was that necessary?"

"No. But it was satisfying."

Ben smirked and shook his head. He motioned with his head for Dexter to follow him. He wanted to be out of earshot of Tito. The last thing he needed was him knowing what he had in mind.

"Okay, here's the thing. There is a strong possibility they aren't going to hand over both of them."

"Well, that's no surprise."

"So we will draw them out. Give them a reason to

think we will deal with him. Lure them out while one of us slips inside and gets the other one."

Dexter's eyebrows shot up. "You are kidding, right?"

"Well do you have a better idea?" He paused and Dexter said nothing. "Think about it logically. It makes sense. Unless you want to go in there guns blazing and risk all of us being killed. There are only a few options we have."

"Options? You only mentioned one. And anyway, who is going in?"

He stared back at him blankly. Dexter clued in and tossed his hands up.

"Oh no, I'm not going in there. Screw that."

"You're a thief, Dexter. You take risks all the time. Besides, my ankle is mangled, you can move faster than I can."

"But not faster than a bullet."

Ben placed his hand on Dexter's shoulder. "He's heard my voice. He'll want to know where I am if I go in instead. I need you to do this. They need you to do this."

Dexter blew out his cheeks and ran a hand around the back of his neck. "How the hell did I wind up with you all? All right just tell me what you want me to do."

"I will bring Tito out into the middle of the road on the basis that we will do an exchange, one for one. At first, I will demand they release both but he's not going to buy that, but he might go for exchanging one."

"Who?"

"Zeke."

"Zeke? Are you kidding me? He's the asshole that got us into this mess."

"Dexter, he didn't know there would be squatters in his home."

"Seriously, Ben, in light all of this end of the world shit. Do you think any of this matters? We are all going to be dead anyway in a matter of hours, days, whatever it might be. Whether we die from a bullet or from an asteroid, I don't think it matters. No, I say we get the hell out of here."

"Really? Are we back to that again? What happened to

"All right just tell me what you want me to do?"

He shrugged. "Ben, this isn't like being asked to take a trip down to the store and pick up a carton of milk. You are expecting me to put my life on the line here."

"You're not the only one. This could go south on us real quick, but unless you have a better idea, this is the best I can think of right now. The longer we wait, the more time they have to figure out an alternative means of getting shit bag over there back."

Dexter looked off in his direction and then back towards Zeke's home. "I don't like this. Not one bit."

"Join the club. The sooner we get this over, the better."

Ben handed over the Desert Eagle handgun to him and told him what he had in mind.

"Don't mess this up," he said before dashing away into the shadows to go around the back of the mansion. Ben watched for a few seconds until he was gone then went back over to where Aamir was.

Tito chuckled. "Where's your friend?"

"Taking a piss, you want to hold it?"

"Fuck you."

Aamir shot him a glance and looked off into the distance. Ben walked over to Tito and grabbed a hold of him and threw him down so they could tie off his hands. Until this point, the only thing protecting them from this asshole was the gun Aamir was holding to the back of his head. He wanted to make damn sure this fool didn't make a run for it. He yanked at the man's shirt sleeve until it tore, then ripped it off his arms and used it to tie off his wrists.

"Shit, man, you're cutting off my circulation."

"You're lucky I don't wrap it around your throat," Ben shot back.

"When I get out of this, you are the first one I'm going to kill."

"Get out? The only way you are getting out of this is with a bullet in your head. Now get up and move." He turned to Aamir and said, "He twitches, shows any sign of attempting to run, or even breathes funny, squeeze the trigger."

They trudged out into the middle of the road and he kicked the back of his knees forcing him to the ground. Tito let out a groan.

"Right, let's get this show on the road." Saying no words he motioned to Aamir to give him the gun. Tito's back was turned so he didn't have to worry about him seeing them take the gun off him. He then brought the barrel up and aimed at one of the windows and fired. It shattered and then he shouted out, "Assholes! Listen up. You want your guy, you have twenty seconds to bring out our friends. Time is ticking. You decide."

He then handed the gun back to Aamir.

* * *

A short distance away under a canopy of trees and darkness, Dexter shuffled along, keeping an eye on the house. His heart was racing. *This is a dumb idea,* he told himself. *Why didn't you stay in Vegas? You could have survived easily without these people. In fact, why don't you go now? Go, run, you've got a gun, you'll be able to find a car and leave these chumps behind. You didn't need them before, and you don't need them now.*

The battle inside his head kept waging as he circled around the back of the home, staying out of sight. Under any other conditions he would have done it but there was something about Felicity's certainty that worried him. He gazed up into the sky. Shouldn't he be able to see an asteroid coming? Wouldn't it loom over the earth, casting a large shadow? Or was that just when it entered the atmosphere? He gritted his teeth and arrived at a spot in a cluster of trees that gave him a good view of the inside of the house. It was lit up, providing him a nice shot of the bikers. They were moving back and forth while Ben was shouting at the top of his voice, counting down from twenty.

His eyes fell upon Felicity. She was on her knees, and a guy had a gun to her head.

C'mon.

"Fourteen, thirteen, twelve," Ben cried out.

He crouched down, hiding behind a large cluster of

sissoo, Chilean mesquite, willow acacia and tipu trees. Slowly but surely two of the men shoved Dexter back out the side door and he could hear them replying to Ben.

"Okay, okay. What do you want?"

"To make an exchange. Your guy for our friends."

"Now that's not a fair exchange. You send on over Tito and we'll send Blackstone back to you."

"No, we want Felicity. You give us both and we will be out of your hair. You can get back to drinking and doing whatever the hell you were doing."

While they continued to argue back and forth, Dexter knew this was it. He tried to pump himself up. He swallowed hard and dashed out of the tree line heading for the back door. Inside he could see the guy still holding a gun on Felicity. He needed to distract him, get the gun away so he could…

His eyes widened. He was ten feet from the French doors when Felicity reacted. Her hands came around and she latched on to the guy's weapon hand and… bit it?

The gun went off, two shots were fired.

In that instant, all hesitation went out the window, this wasn't going to plan but he kind of figured they weren't just going to get them back without encountering a few hiccups. Dexter burst in the back door and had no other choice but to fire a round into the back of the biker as he was beating on Felicity's face with his other hand trying to get her to let go. She was like a wild animal, holding on for dear life.

The bullet punctured his back and brought him down hard.

He knew within seconds the other two would burst through the front door to find out what the hell was going on, so he circled around the area that led into the kitchen and waited for them. Out the corner of his eye, he saw Felicity grab the gun from the biker and bolt out the back door. It was chaotic and everything was happening in a matter of seconds. At the precise moment, she disappeared out the back, one of them came in the side door, shouting, "Doc?"

Great, she's gone, now I'm stuck in here with them.

The biker rushed by him and without giving it another thought he raised the Eagle and squeezed off two rounds dropping the second guy. The first guy he dropped was still alive and groaning on the ground beneath his dead pal.

Sweating and fully expecting the next guy to come in, he pressed his back to the door and waited. But he didn't enter. Probably had more sense than the other two.

* * *

Outside, Ben had heard the commotion, he watched as the guy who Tito referred to as Mac sent in his pal.

"If he doesn't come out, your friend here is as good as dead."

Zeke was on the ground, his hands behind his head, and Mac had a clump of his hair in his hand and was holding the gun against the back of his head, mirroring what Aamir was doing with Tito. A few tense minutes passed, the sound of more gunfire erupted and he could only imagine what was going on inside the house.

"Doc, Ricky?" he shouted over his shoulder while

keeping a close eye on Ben. What he didn't see was Felicity coming out of the trees off to his right. She came out bearing a Glock in her hand.

"Give me the gun, Aamir," Ben said.

"What?"

"Now."

Aamir handed it to him and he took over holding it to Tito's head.

"Put it down," Felicity said. Mac turned, a look of shock on his face. He shook his head.

"Ricky? Doc?"

"They're probably dead, Mac, shoot him!" Tito shouted.

"Shut the fuck up," Ben said before swiping him across the back of the head with the handgun.

Mac backed up, dragging Zeke by his long hair. His handgun raked back and forth between Ben and Felicity. "I will fucking end his life. Put it down." He then pressed the gun to the back of Zeke's head and continued to yell as he stepped back heading for the house. "I swear, you shoot me, I will squeeze this trigger and it's all over."

Zeke throughout the whole thing was crying like a bitch, telling them to put their guns down. But that wouldn't happen.

No sooner had Mac made it within five feet of the door he'd previously exited, than a gun echoed. One final round, and Mac dropped. Coming into view a few seconds later was Dexter, holding a gun out in front of him.

"It's over. They're all dead."

He lowered his gun and Ben forced Tito to get up and walk towards the house. Zeke was lying on his face still blubbering until he saw Dexter. He jumped up and with tears coming down his face, he slammed into Dexter pinning him against the wall.

"You nearly cost me my life."

Felicity hurried over and pulled him back. "Zeke, get off him."

"Cost you your life? You self-righteous asshole!" Dexter said. "You put all of us in jeopardy. Oh, you had to come here. You had to be the big shot and show us your mansion. Well, you know what, I saved your damn life. Be grateful! If it had been my decision, I would have left you to die. You have Ben and me to thank for being alive right now. So back the fuck up." Dexter shouted so loudly in his face, spit was coming out of his mouth.

The glow of the light revealed that Zeke had pissed himself out of fear.

Zeke walked a short distance away and Felicity went over to him to thank him for coming to her aid. Ben could see he was still trembling. Aamir went inside while Ben kept a firm grip on Tito. Tito's tune soon changed when Aamir came out and told him that one of them was still alive inside but barely.

"What should we do with him?" Aamir asked.

"Please. You don't have to kill me. I'm sorry, I will leave, you will never see me again."

Ben stared at him for a few seconds, and he watched as Zeke went inside the house.

"You know this could have all been avoided if you had

just shown some decency."

"I know. I'm sorry."

"Yeah, I bet you are."

Ben brought up the gun to the back of his head and Tito squeezed his eyes shut waiting for the sound of the gun. However, when a single shot echoed, it hadn't come from Ben's piece, it came from the house. Aamir sprinted to the door and looked inside just as Zeke came out holding a .45 Magnum. Without saying a word, he leveled it at Tito and fired. The eruption and suddenness startled them all.

Once the round was fired, Zeke turned and walked back into the house.

The rest of them stood there, looking down at Tito's body and allowing the moment to sink in. The events in Vegas had upheaved their lives and brought them together, but this had taken them over an invisible line and would change them forever.

Chapter 20

The underground base was buzzing with activity when Charlie returned. Though his head hung heavy, he couldn't endanger the lives of the pilot and lieutenant any more than he already had. As the rotors slowed and Harley hopped out of the bird, he was met by his wife and two kids. They rushed up to meet him and wrapped their arms around him. The pilot who went by the name Davis, was met by his girlfriend.

Davis looked back at him before he walked away.

"Doctor Meyer," Harley said breaking away from his family. "I'm sorry."

"I appreciate you trying."

"If we had more time, and fuel, I would have been more than willing to search but…"

"Don't mention it."

Charlie headed back inside, checking his phone messages as he went. There was still nothing. He listened to the first one that Felicity had left just so he could hear her voice again. Losing Kathy had almost killed him, but the thought of his daughter out there troubled him even more.

"Charlie, any luck?" William said appearing off to his side through a doorway.

He shook his head and William placed his hand on his shoulder to console him. "I know this isn't what you want to hear but I will say it, anyway. Don't beat yourself up over this. You tried."

"Did I?" Charlie said. "Because I don't think I tried hard enough. I should have stayed there."

"We can't afford to lose you."

"Because I offer humanity something? Please, you are buying into your own press, William."

"Charlie, we leave in seventy-two hours."

With that said he walked away, returning to his room to take a shower and wash off the grime of the day. William's words only intensified the stress he was feeling. His gut churned and the memory of his daughter's voice made him hate himself even more.

* * *

Zeke sniffed a few lines of coke and no one stopped him. In fact, everyone said little for the next hour. Felicity had given Dexter a hand dragging out the bodies from the house, after that they helped themselves to a variety of canned food, and Ben went through the house searching for a duffel bag to fill up with supplies they could take with them.

For the most part, it was basic stuff, the kind of gear that might have been found in a bug-out bag. They only took the essentials; something for shelter like black plastic bags to keep the rain off, blankets and sleeping bags, and items to start a fire like a Zippo lighter, flint and steel. They would have taken a water filtration kit but Zeke had none. When Aamir asked why, he grunted and went back to snorting a line of coke.

"Here, toss this in," Ben said after finding a first-aid kit, along with a knife and a pair of pliers. They then gathered together some fresh clothes, and entered the garage to see if there was any cord or flashlights. Felicity and Ben went from room to room gathering as much as they could fit inside that bag. Toiletries were one of the last things they collected, including toilet paper, soap, deodorant, moist towelettes, and toothpaste. There was no telling how long they would be on the road and whether they would have the time to gather more items from stores. Within the first seventy-two hours, stores would be looted and stripped bare.

"What about communication?" Aamir said. "We could have used that tonight."

"Zeke, you got any two-way radios?"

"Why the hell would I have that? I own a phone."

"Yeah, and a fat lot of good that is doing us."

"Well, I'm sorry I don't live my life thinking the end of the world is about to happen." He pulled out a cigarette and lit it.

"We can probably find a store."

"A store, of course, products… no."

Once they had gathered as much as they could, all of

them used some of the bottled water that Zeke had to clean themselves. Though it was freezing cold, getting rid of the grime felt good. Felicity ended up wearing a pair of Zeke's pants and shirt. It was too big, so she had to roll up the sleeves and pant legs but at least it was clean.

While she was getting dressed, she noticed Dexter was looking at her through the door. He wasn't doing it on purpose but was laying on one of the beds and happened to look over. She shut the door and smirked. He wasn't a bad-looking guy, but her mind was far from that. Men were the last thing on her mind even though she was surrounded by them.

When she came out, he looked her up and down.

"Not bad."

"What, now or before?"

"Both."

He smiled and hopped up, about to head into the bathroom and get cleaned up.

"Dexter."

He cast a glance over his shoulder. "Yeah?"

"I appreciate what you did earlier. Coming back for us I mean."

He shrugged and his lip curled up before he closed the door behind him.

Felicity headed back into the living area where Ben and Aamir were in a discussion about the evening. It had affected them all in different ways. How could they not be? It wasn't like killing people was an everyday occurrence. Though it had only been Zeke and Dexter doing the killing, they all knew that the chances of them encountering more threats on the road were high.

"So you are saying you wouldn't have killed him?" Ben asked.

"I didn't think about it. I was just doing what you told me."

"But if he had turned on you?"

"I…" Aamir looked down.

Felicity took a seat nearby and drank the rest of her drink.

"We need to head out soon. Zeke, where's your

landline phone?"

He motioned down the hall. "First room on the right."

She snagged up an apple and headed down. She would try to phone her father again. Inside the room, it was a simple office. A shelf full of books about magic, a few awards on the walls, two photos of him from his glory days in TV. She took a seat behind the thick mahogany table and lifted the receiver. It was working.

She closed her eyes and thanked God. Though she wasn't a religious person her mother had tried to teach her about spirituality. She said it was something that everyone at some point would have to decide for themselves.

"Felicity, we come into this world alone and for the most part, we will leave it alone. In between that time, you will have some highs and lows. Anyone can make it through the highs, but the lows, they can be awfully lonely if you don't have something to put your trust in."

For the longest time she believed the same way as her mother until she got cancer, after that, she had cast her beliefs aside. Though, now, after all that had happened and all that could happen, she was thinking that having some higher power on her side might be best.

Felicity dialed the number and once again got his voicemail. She left another message and then hung up, though this time leaving Zeke's home number which was scribbled down on a pad of paper with a list of numbers.

She sat back in the rich leather seat and looked around. In front of her were several photos, she leaned forward and picked them up. They were of different kids. As she was looking at them, Zeke walked up to the door. She met his gaze, and he came in and leaned against the shelving unit.

"These your kids?"

He nodded while smoking. He looked more at ease now.

"Have you ever seen them, I mean since they were born?"

"Yes and no. The one in Florida, I have, his name is Adam. Until he was six he lived here and then his mother returned to Florida to live with her parents after we separated. I miss him every day. The others not so much. Sounds awful, doesn't it?"

"So you've never met them?"

He nodded. "Like I see their faces but that connection is just not there, at least not like with Adam. I've been there several times over the years to take him out but his mother put a stop to that. She said it wasn't good for Adam. That I wasn't a good influence and that it was making it hard for his new stepfather, Clyde, to bond with him."

"But you are his father."

"Exactly. She doesn't see it that way. Maggie was always a pain in the ass."

"How did you meet her?"

He eyed Felicity. "This will sound bad. But I met her in a strip joint. She was a stripper. We got on really well at first."

"I bet you did," she replied taking a bite of her apple.

"No, not in that way… Well, kind of in that way at

first. But after, we had a lot in common. She was an entrepreneur. She wanted to start her own business and whatnot. So I helped her. I had the money back then."

"So why did she leave you?"

He shrugged. "Why does anyone leave? We get tired of each other, we get bored, we wake up one day and realize that we don't recognize the person we're sleeping across from, or we don't like the reflection in the mirror." He took a puff of his cigarette. "That's life, as they would say."

"He has your eyes," Felicity said.

"You think?"

She was just about to say something when the phone rang. There wasn't even a second of hesitation before she scooped it up. "Dad?"

"Felicity?" She heard him sigh with relief. "Oh my God."

"I… I thought you were dead."

"No, I'm very much alive. Where are you? I came. I showed up at the Mirage."

"What?"

"I got a pilot to bring me out, but you were gone."

"We had to leave. I'm with a group of survivors."

"Where?"

"Southeast of Las Vegas. In Henderson." She paused for a second. "Dad, it's bad here. Um, I got your messages." She paused. "Is an asteroid on its way?"

There was silence on the other end of the phone.

"Dad."

"Yes."

"How long have we got?"

"Estimation, about seventy-two hours."

She exhaled hard. "Even if we drove fast and didn't stop, it would take us thirty-five hours but with the state of the country right now, it could take twice, even three times as long as that. Hell, I don't even know if we could get there. The car we have only has a certain amount of gas."

"Listen, I will try to see if I can get them to give me the helicopter one more time. Can you hang tight where you are? I'll call right back."

"Okay."

"And Felicity."

"Yeah?"

"I'm so sorry for everything that has happened between you and me. I love you. I mean that."

"I know you do, Dad. I love you too."

She hung up and leaned back in the chair.

"So?" Zeke asked. "Are we in?"

"That depends. Are you still coming?"

He gazed down at the floor. "I imagine they don't have many magicians, right?"

"Probably not," she smirked.

He grinned. "People always need entertainment."

* * *

Charlie hurried down the corridor. It had been the first good bit of news he'd received since the shit Storm of the Century had kicked off. Though he felt elated to know his daughter was alive, he knew this would not be easy. William spun around as he came sprinting into the room and reeled off his request.

"Slow down, Charlie, calm down. What is up?"

"Felicity. She's alive. I spoke with her."

"That's good. Real good."

"So all we need is to get Lieutenant Harley or even just Davis to take me back out to Vegas and I can pick her up. I know where she is now."

"Charlie. You said you knew where she was last time."

"William, I know, but that was different. She's waiting there for me, last time she didn't know if I had got her phone message."

William sucked in air and leaned back in his chair.

"From one friend to another, please."

"Give me a second," William said turning and grabbing a phone. Charlie slapped his hands together. "Yes! Yes!" he repeated. "This is good, very good."

William glanced up at him as he spoke into the phone.

"Yeah, can you tell me where Lieutenant Harley is?"

There was silence and William nodded a few times. "Right. Okay. Sure thing."

He hung up and slowly turned around and already Charlie was not liking the look on his face. "A bit of a problem, Charlie. The LT is unavailable at the moment."

"Well, get him on the line. I want to speak to him."

"He's evacuating more of those on the list."

Charlie shifted his weight and ran two hands through his hair. "So when's he back?"

"No ETA on that."

"Then give me someone else."

"There is no one else, Charlie. We are already maxed out. You were lucky to get the LT for the short period of time that you did. I'm afraid it's not happening."

"It has to happen. She's out there, I'm not leaving her."

William nodded. He knew this was a touchy situation.

"I don't know what to suggest, Charlie. We are down to the wire here and some of the people on the list haven't even been located yet, which means all our guys will be out there for quite some time. Maybe, um, if she tried heading this way..."

He was quick to cut him off. "You really have no idea what it's like out there, do you?"

William shrugged.

"See, this is what I'm talking about. Government sits back in the safety of their kingdom while the rest of the world is suffering out there."

"Charlie."

"Don't Charlie me."

He turned and exited the door and returned to his room to place a call to his daughter. His mind was turning over. He felt sick to his stomach from worry. The phone rang once and Felicity picked up.

"Dad."

"Hi, honey."

"So?"

"We have a problem on this end."

"What do you mean?"

"I can't get a pilot to head out. At least I can't right now."

There was silence as both of them contemplated what

that meant.

"So we are on our own."

He didn't want to say yes, but that was the reality.

"You know we aren't going to make it in time," Felicity said.

"Don't say that. It's not over yet."

She breathed in deeply. "What are their plans?"

"They've created a ship called *Deliverance* that can hold one hundred thousand people. They have already begun sending up shuttles. We have less than seventy-two hours until the asteroid hits."

"Right."

She went quiet, then finally spoke.

"I'm sorry, Dad, for not getting back to you. I should have listened about that shithead boyfriend of mine and well..."

"You listen here, Felicity. I'm not giving up. Get your ass in a car and head towards Cape Canaveral. As soon as I can get a Black Hawk up in the air, we will come and get you. Do you understand?"

She chuckled. "Always the optimist."

Chapter 21

The SUV only got them about two hundred miles before they had to get out and walk somewhere near Flagstaff. Vast crevices, stalled vehicles and mounds of debris covered the roads and had taken down trees that blocked their pathway. To say it was disheartening would have been an understatement. Zeke cursed for close to twenty minutes non-stop after they abandoned the SUV and continued to Flagstaff by foot.

Trails of rocks had rolled down from the mountains like an avalanche turning the landscape into a field of boulders.

"We'll keep going by foot until we find another vehicle. You had to know this would happen."

Zeke dropped another F-bomb.

"At least we're still alive," Aamir said.

They all swung back and forth between being positive and negative.

The journey from Vegas to Flagstaff under normal conditions would have taken them close to four hours, it had taken an additional hour due to all the swerving, and detours they had to take.

"There is no way in hell we will get to Cape Canaveral in less than seventy-two hours. We are screwed," Zeke muttered. "I would have been better off staying at home. At least there I could have finished my final hours in the lap of luxury. Here, I'm sweating my balls off, thirsty and my legs are killing me," he yelled adding emphasis.

"Here, take this," Dexter said pulling out a bottle of water from his backpack. Zeke's eyes widened.

"What the hell? Are you telling me you have had that in your pack all this time?"

He shrugged. "Of course, didn't you hear us when we said pack your bag with bottles of water?"

"I couldn't carry more than two bottles. It would have been too heavy."

"And that's my problem? Do you want it or not?" He put his hand out and offered it to him. Zeke scowled and went to snatch it out of his hands when Dexter yanked it back.

"Well tough shit! It's mine." With that said he unscrewed the top, chugged back on it until it was half empty and then poured the rest over his head while staring up at the burning sun beating down on them.

"Are you kidding me?"

Dexter tossed the empty bottle at him and walked past. Zeke kicked the bottle across the ground and put some distance between him and the rest of them.

"Dexter, was that necessary?" Felicity asked.

"Do I even need to answer that?"

As they came over a rise in the road which led down into Flagstaff, their eyes looked on at the devastation. It too hadn't fared well. A huge city in the state of Arizona, it was surrounded by mountains and ponderosa pine forests but now a person would have been hard-pressed to tell what it was. It was like someone had swallowed up the center of the city.

"That looks a helluva lot like an impact site."

"Poor bastards. Probably didn't know."

"At least their death would have been quick," Aamir said before muttering a prayer under his breath. At a glance, it looked like someone had dropped a large rock into a lake and ripples had spread outward. There were ripples of debris, homes, stores, vehicles piled up on top of each other, like a huge junkyard. Bodies were everywhere. Fires still flared up into the sky and thick billows of smoke drifted aimlessly across the ruined landscape, carried by the wind. Felicity had never seen so many dead people in one place.

"Cover your faces," Felicity said. "There's no telling what poisonous fumes are in the air." That was the thing about a natural disaster. It had a domino effect. If people were not killed by the initial meteor shower, earthquakes and volcanic eruptions, what followed could suffocate them. Heavy toxic smoke from burned plastic and chemicals would have been carried far and wide. Those trapped and alive beneath rubble would have been the first to succumb, then anyone who didn't get away from the city would have been next.

"I want to stop here, get something to drink," Zeke said.

"We can't. We have to keep moving."

"Are you out of your mind? Do you honestly think I will trudge for seventy-two hours, non-stop? Even if I could, I wouldn't do it. No, your father told you we were to contact him in every major city by landline. Who knows, by now he might have obtained another Black Hawk. Heck, we could just put our feet up here and wait for them to show up."

"Or we could keep on walking," Dexter said brushing past him.

"Has anyone told you what a pain in the ass you are?" Zeke said hurrying to catch up with Dexter.

"All the time."

"And?"

"I ignored them, like I'm doing with you. You see that's the difference between me and you, Zekey boy. I admit I'm a pain in the ass, you don't. I ignore comments from the peanut gallery, you don't. I remain poised, calm and collected, you don't."

"Okay, okay, I get it. It's all bullshit but I get it."

Dexter laughed as they trudged down in near silence, barely saying anything to one another. Comments were only filled with grumbles or jabs at Zeke for whining. Felicity looked on at the city of Flagstaff, and her heart sank. At one time it had been home to the San Francisco Peaks and had bragging rights for having the tallest mountain in the state, and the popular Arizona Snowbowl ski resort but now… everything was gray and dismal looking.

Ash still drifted in the air like huge snowflakes. Aamir said it was probably from Sunset Crater Volcano. They'd had an eruption scare back in 2015 when satellite images reported steam rising from the crater, but it turned out the steam was from a forest fire. According to geologists, the volcano was supposed to be extinct, so they figured the ash was coming from buildings on fire.

The entire town looked like a house of cards just

waiting to collapse.

"Be careful where you walk," Dexter said after nearly slipping.

It felt like they were walking down inside a huge bowl where at the center was a mammoth sinkhole. However, they could see from the fire it was more likely one of several impact sites. Felicity climbed over scattered cars, and squeezed through tight openings in structures that had partially crumbled. Debris from falling buildings had trapped many people inside vehicles. As they walked past one, they saw a dead baby in the back, still strapped in its car seat. Its skin was covered with a thin layer of dust, and shards of glass. Whoever was in the front didn't stand a chance as a corner of a bank had pulverized the metal, flattening the front. They could hear the fire crackling and the air was thick with black smoke.

Dexter was leading the way when suddenly he tossed up a hand to alert the others. They'd all agreed after the shit they went through with the bikers back in Henderson, the last thing they wanted was more trouble, so they'd come up with a form of communicating. Ben said it was from his days in the military, but Aamir called him out on it, and eventually, he caved and said it was from watching one too many war movies. It intrigued Felicity that despite all that had happened, people still tried to prove their worth by lying. Ben didn't see it that way, he said he would string them along for a while and then tell them but none of them bought it.

They all dropped low and remained still while Dexter peered around a crushed van. He shuffled over to the rest of them and in a low voice spoke, "There's three of them. They look like regular folk to me but they are armed. What do you want to do?"

"I vote we send you out while we backtrack and circle around and keep on moving," Zeke said with a smile on his face. "Being as you enjoy killing people."

Dexter flipped him the bird. "I killed two, so did you."

"Are you two done with your pissing match?" Felicity asked. "Let me take a look."

She stayed in a crouched position and slipped past

Zeke up to the side of the van. Sure enough, about sixty feet away, three individuals dressed in hunting gear were rooting through the front of a store. She turned back and considered their options. Realistically, backtracking and circling around would only slow them down but then so was getting caught in a precarious position with armed individuals. Though not everyone would be like the bikers, they still had to be careful. She made her way back to the others.

"We need to decide on this together. I will not be held responsible for deciding and then everything goes wrong."

"Oh no?" Zeke asked. "Aren't we out here because of your decision?"

She pointed a finger at him. "You made that decision. Not me."

He grumbled again.

"I've got an idea," Ben said. "Just be prepared to engage with them if things go south."

He reached down and scooped up handfuls of ash and rubbed it all over his clothes and then dumped more of it over his head.

"What are you doing?" Aamir asked.

"Watch and learn, little man," he said before tucking a Glock into the back of his pants and then getting up.

"Ben," Felicity said.

"Don't worry."

He headed out from around the vehicle, groaning excessively. Felicity shuffled up to the side and peered around. Ben staggered and stumbled a few times giving one hell of a performance as he veered around the obstacle course of destruction and made his way towards the figures.

"Help, please."

The three strangers turned and stared at him for a few seconds. One of them cast his eyes around nervously and muttered something to the other two before rushing towards Ben. Felicity heard the sound of Zeke's gun cocking in preparation.

"That's far enough," the man said. He was covered from head to toe in camouflage hunting gear. All three of them looked as if they had just stepped right out of the wilderness.

"I just need water."

"Anyone else with you?"

"No, just me," Ben replied.

"You carrying?"

There was a moment of hesitation by Ben before he nodded.

"Pull it out and toss it over here."

"Don't do it," Dexter muttered under his breath. As Ben went to reach for his weapon, the guy raised his rifle and for a split second, tension hung in the air.

"I'm just gonna lower it, okay?"

Ben kept one hand up while the other reached for the gun and placed it down on the ground. He then kicked it over.

"Oh my God, what an idiot!" Dexter muttered. Felicity had to agree, there was no way in hell she would have handed her weapon over. And by the sounds of the mumbling from Aamir and Zeke, they were in agreement too. But that was to be expected from traveling with all types of people. Not everyone thought the same. Stupidity to one was tactics to another. They immediately realized that within seconds of him kicking over the gun.

The camo dude reached down and picked it up.

"Where's the magazine?"

"There wasn't one."

"If you're lying or going to try anything, I'm warning you now, I will shoot you."

His head shifted from side to side. They could tell all three of them were nervous and on their guard. Ben nodded in response to what the guy said.

"All right, come on."

He waved him over and Ben shuffled towards them.

"I say we do this now, kill all three of them," Dexter muttered.

"Wait," Felicity answered.

Once the guy had a hand on Ben, he brought him over to the other two and one of them pulled out a canister and handed it to him. They watched in silence as he chugged it back and then another one offered him a cigarette.

"Well, I'll be damned. There are good people left."

They remained in that spot until Ben must have told them he wasn't alone. At first, it caused them to back up and yell at him but he put his hands up and convinced them they wouldn't harm anyone.

"Come on out!" Ben shouted waving to them. Slowly but surely they emerged from behind the vehicle.

"Put that gun away," Felicity muttered to Zeke. "We don't want to give them any more reason to kill us than they already have."

All three of them kept their weapons trained on Aamir, Zeke and the other two as they made their way over.

"You want to lower your rifles? If we wanted you dead, you already would be by now," Dexter said.

"Throw over your weapons."

"That's not going to happen," Felicity piped up. "Now like my friend said, if we wanted you dead, we could have taken the shot by now. We need to rest for a few minutes, find more supplies and then we will be on our way."

They remained at a good distance from them in case they changed their mind.

"Where you from?"

"Vegas but we're heading for Florida."

One of them chuckled. "That's a long way. Why are you heading there?"

"Family," Felicity said before any of the others mentioned the real reason.

They eyed them and continued to scan the surroundings.

"It's just us. In case you're wondering."

"That's what he said before you all showed your faces. Why should I believe you?"

Felicity had enough of this. "Look, we don't have a lot of time so if you plan on shooting us, go ahead but I'm unarmed. Now we have two more weapons but that is it. I'm going to make my way over to where you are, okay? I'm tired and have had one hell of a day."

With that said, she stepped forward, and she heard the

sound of their rifles as the men shifted their weight. Once she made it over she smiled. “See. Not everyone is bad.”

“And the others?”

Felicity turned. “Come on, guys.”

Dexter tucked the Desert Eagle into his waistband and walked over. Zeke was the last to join them but he refused to put his gun away. He eyed them as suspiciously as they did him. Fortunately, no one got up in each other’s faces.

“You guys from here?” Felicity asked after accepting water from them.

“Just on the outskirts of town. I’m Ethan, this is Thomas and…” Before he finished the other one tore off the mask and hood that was covering her face and answered. Long flowing blond hair fell down beyond her shoulders. “I’m Kira.”

“They’re my family,” Ethan said.

Chapter 22

It became obvious fairly quickly that they were in a hurry. "Have you by any chance come across a landline phone that is working?"

"What do you need that for?" Ethan asked, as they sat around drinking water and chomping on granola bars.

"Contact family."

Ethan studied her face.

"What do you know about what's happened?" Felicity asked.

"Only what we've seen. We have a cabin in the woods, we live off the grid and after my wife didn't return from town, and the meteor hit, all hell broke loose. That's what we're doing down here, trying to find her."

She cast a glance at Kira and Thomas. His son and daughter were in their late teens.

"This meteor shower is part of a precursor to something far worse. There is an asteroid that is heading towards the planet. When it hits, life, as we know it, will be wiped out. This is nothing compared to what is coming."

"That's fine, I have a bunker. Yep, we stocked up on enough to survive six months with all the problems that have been happening with Korea and whatnot."

His kids nodded and smiled and she couldn't help feel sorry for them.

"I'm afraid, it won't be good enough," she replied. "We're heading to Florida because my father works with the government. They have a plan to take 100,000 people to an airship in space."

"It's called *Deliverance*," Dexter piped up. He was lying on his side smoking a cigarette and looking a lot more relaxed than he was ten minutes earlier.

Ethan stared blankly at her before looking down into his hand and rolling around his wedding band on his finger.

"You can come with us. I'm sure there is more than enough room."

"That's kind of you but we will remain here."

Zeke spat out his drink and tapped Dexter on the leg. "And you thought I was mad," he said before chuckling. He had a way of putting his foot in his mouth at the worst times.

"My wife is out there, somewhere. I want to find her, give her a proper burial."

"Are you frigging kidding me? She's already buried," Zeke said.

"Right, that's it. Get up, let's go," Dexter said grabbing a hold of Zeke and pulling him away from the group. They went a distance and started arguing. It was becoming the norm. Though Felicity kind of figured why Dexter was tearing into him. Zeke just didn't have an off switch. It was like he lived in a different world. There was no compassion. No thought was given to what came out of his mouth. He said whatever the hell he liked.

Ethan reached down and took a handful of ash and then tossed it away. "I know it sounds odd but the good Lord knew about this and well, if this is how it's meant to end, then so be it. I would rather die here. In my hometown with my kids and my wife."

Though Felicity understood the part about being with family, she struggled to understand why anyone would willingly perish when there was a separate door they could walk through.

"And what about you guys?" Felicity asked, posing the question to Thomas and Kira. They looked at their father, their faces despondent, perhaps resigned to the fate he'd decided for them.

"If my father is staying, so am I," Thomas said.

"Me too," Kira added.

Ethan reached over and gripped their hands and gave a strong smile.

"You need not worry about us, Felicity. The lord has taken good care of us and given me more in the few years I've been on this planet than some get in a whole lifetime. What you need to understand is that when my wife was here, we lived our lives somewhat separate from the rest of society. We kept to ourselves, hunted for food, fished and only came down to the town for medicine, guns and a few supplies. That's the way we choose to live, and that's the way we will choose to die. Now don't get me wrong, I don't want to die, but I don't fear death. Eventually, we all die. It's as natural as breathing. I didn't worry before I was born, and I will not worry about it now," he said before taking a swig from a canister of water.

"Now we can help you gather some extra supplies, hell, we might even be able to find a vehicle that you can use but we will stay."

Felicity nodded. "The option is there."

"I appreciate that."

He got up, cutting short the conversation. "There is a motel about three miles from here that hasn't collapsed. They probably have a phone in there." He turned to Thomas and whispered something and he shot off towards a cluster of crumbled buildings.

"Have you seen any other survivors?" Ben asked.

"Besides us? Sure. Not everyone was wiped out. There are others like us who live in the mountains but here in town, no, we haven't seen anyone."

"Guess it makes sense."

"Come, we'll get you a few supplies and send you on your way."

They'd spent only about fifteen minutes with them but in that short time, Felicity felt a connection to them. It was strange how a natural disaster could bring humanity together and yet tear them apart. This group was the complete opposite of the bikers. Instead of taking in times of scarcity, they were giving. It restored her hope in humanity again.

Thomas reappeared carrying a large brown burlap sack over his shoulder. He jogged and hopped over debris making his way back. Once he reached them he dumped the bag down and Ethan fished inside and pulled out cans of fruit, granola bars and bottles of water. He handed them off and each of them stuffed their backpack with as much as they could carry.

"Thank you, Ethan."

"It's the least I can do."

"What about a vehicle?"

"I can't work miracles, only the lord can do that but on the road that heads out of this town towards the motel, there is a used auto dealership. We passed it on the way in. It's in one hell of a state, but there were a few vehicles intact. You will probably need some gas though. I can't help you with that but I'm sure you'll figure something out."

After they had gathered together what they needed, Felicity leaned in and hugged Ethan.

"I hope you find your wife."

"I hope so too."

He offered back a warm smile, and she gave the kids a hug before turning to leave. As they parted ways she couldn't help feeling sad. Even though Ethan said he was content with whatever came their way that didn't mean he wasn't fearful. How many others would resign to their fate? How many would even know until the final few seconds? No matter how humanity was divided in life, there was one thing they were all on the same page about

— family. It was the one thing that was most important.

As they trudged on out of the city, leaving behind the ruins, Felicity thought about her own mother. In many ways, she was pleased she didn't have to endure this or see what she'd made of her life. She would have probably died from the shock.

"I'm telling you, its religious nonsense. You heard the guy, the lord this, the lord that. Honestly, where the hell is the lord when all of this happened? Let me guess, he was snoozing," Zeke said puffing away on a cigarette.

"Just because you don't understand it, doesn't mean a deity is not behind it and doing what is best for humanity," Aamir said.

"Oh please, put a sock in it, Aamir. If you are going to give me a sermon on the mount, I don't want to hear it."

"I'm not a Christian, I'm Hindu."

"And like that makes it any better."

Dexter had this puzzled look on his face and had remained quiet the whole time Zeke was droning on about his distaste for religion and how it only appealed to simple-minded people or those with problems who couldn't solve them themselves. Eventually, though he chimed in.

"So you don't have a religion, then, Zeke?"

"Nope," he said making this popping sound with his mouth.

"And you don't believe in a God?"

"Nope."

"So why have you got that cross around your neck?"

"It's bling."

They all laughed and Dexter shook his head.

"What?" Zeke asked, not seeing the funny side to it.

"What about you, Felicity? You a believer?" Dexter asked.

"What is this, Sunday?" Zeke asked. "Can we stop talking about this?"

"Does it get under your skin, Zeke?"

He scowled at him.

"Actually I've never been a religious person. Though I attended church when I was a kid. I believe there is someone out there. A higher power if you want to call it but I'm just not sure it's what we have all been taught."

"So you think we have got some skewed version."

"Something like that," Felicity said stopping in her tracks. "There it is. The auto dealership." She broke into a jog. The farther they moved away from the city, the clearer the roads became. Not everyone would have got out, and those that had either made it or were swallowed up in the large fissures of crevices that spread across the landscape.

As she weaved her way through the rubble, and leaped over smaller crevices, she was about eight feet from the dealership when the ground gave out from below her. Whether it was a sinkhole, or what, there was no time to register it. In an instant her body was flung downward, and she landed hard, knocking the wind out of her.

Felicity groaned and reached for her ribs which felt broken. Every breath she took in was more painful than the last.

"Felicity!"

She heard their voices but couldn't see a damn thing except for dust and dirt, twisted pieces of vehicles and bodies. All around her covered in a thick layer of dust were dead bodies. In fact, the only things stopping her from slipping farther down into the dark crack in the earth were four vehicles that were jammed sideways, and bodies.

She squinted and rubbed a hand over her dirt-covered face before rolling over and looking up towards the light.

"Hang tight, we're gonna find something to get you out."

She raised a thumb but was unsure if they could see her. She coughed a few times and covered the lower half of her face. Her entire body was engulfed in a plume of dust. When she'd landed the vehicle had shifted beneath her. Now every move she made caused it to creak.

As she lay there, her mind went back to the day she left for Vegas.

The heated argument she had with her father, and her boyfriend hitting her father as he tried to stop them from heading off.

"You will ruin your life, Felicity."

"Maybe I will but it's my life."

Back then she was so angry all the time. After her mother had passed, she felt as if she had taken on the role of her mother. She did everything her mother did, paid the bills, cooked meals, cleaned up, and somewhere in it all she still had to find time to have a life of her own. The problem was after her mother's death, her father had just fallen to pieces. Though unlike others who might hide away for a year in their home, he had thrown himself into his work. So when she finally got the nerve to tell him she was leaving and heading off to Vegas to get married, he didn't know how to deal with it. Instead, he flew off the handle, said things he didn't mean in the heat of the moment, even though he was right about that jerk of a boyfriend.

Her mind snapped back into the present moment just

as a hook with a thick strap plunked down beside her. It bounced a few times against the side of the crevice before she could tell what it was. It looked like they had tied together straps that were used on the back of trucks.

"Do you see it, Felicity?"

"I got it," she muttered reaching over and taking a hold of it.

Slowly they pulled her up, a feat that wasn't easy to do because she had little strength left in her body. The pain in her side was horrendous.

Zeke's and Dexter's faces came into view first, she reached up and Ben clamped onto her hand and pulled her over the lip onto the asphalt. She breathed out hard and remained there for a few minutes more until she could catch her breath.

"Anything broke?"

"My will," she said without breaking a smile. "My left leg hurts but it's my ribs I'm worried about."

She was breathing shallow because each breath she took hurt like hell.

"Can you get up?"

She staggered to her feet and kept one hand over her ribs.

"We should probably get that looked at," Zeke said. "Take your top off."

"Yeah, forget it, buddy, this is not an invitation for a peek show."

"I didn't mean that."

"Forget it, let's just find a vehicle and get on the road. We've wasted enough time in this town as it is. Aamir, how long we got left?"

"We've been on the road for close to four and a half hours."

She let out a heavy sigh, and they went around the opening in the earth and made their way over to the dealership. Only three vehicles had not been destroyed — an old Ford truck, a Chrysler sedan, and a compact Hyundai.

Glass crunched beneath their feet as they made their way inside the dealership and Aamir went off to find keys for the vehicles.

"I always wanted to just take a vehicle without paying for it," Dexter muttered, running his hands over a crushed vehicle. The entire ceiling had collapsed in one area and a huge chunk of concrete had gone through the windshield.

"I bet you did," Zeke replied.

"Here we go again," Aamir muttered.

"I'll check the Ford," Dexter said. They went to the different vehicles and checked to see if they started. All three did. They spent the next fifteen minutes siphoning out gas from multiple vehicles, using a tube from the garage and a bucket, and then they filled up the truck.

Felicity slipped into the truck and lay back allowing the heat from the vents to calm her. She was grateful for the small things, for that was all they had left.

Dexter veered out, and they were back on the road again towards the next city, or for however long the road would take them before another blockade.

Chapter 23

The flea-ridden motel that existed three miles outside of Flagstaff yielded nothing. Ethan wasn't lying, there was a phone, but it was no longer working.

They drove a hundred and eight miles before they had to veer off and get more gas. The journey to Cape Canaveral would take them through countless towns, along with major cities including Albuquerque, Amarillo and Dallas.

They took turns driving and while the others slept. There was one passenger awake at all times to act as a second set of eyes on the road. The problem was there was so much debris on the road it was tough to tell where crevices were until they were practically on them.

The low fuel indicator dinged as they rolled through Gallup, a small city in New Mexico, about three hours from Flagstaff. It was one of the first towns they had arrived at where only a few of the buildings had collapsed.

Many of the structures were still standing.

It was also there they encountered a major setback.

"Hey guys, wake up!" Dexter said putting a hand over and shaking Aamir and Zeke. Felicity had dozed off even though she was meant to be focusing on the road. As she looked out, there were several police vehicles ahead, and an officer holding a shotgun. He put out a hand and Dexter eased off the gas.

When the truck rolled up beside him, Dexter brought the window down.

"Where are you all coming from?"

"Vegas."

"Where are you heading?"

"Florida."

His eyes roamed their faces.

"Driver's license and registration."

"I would love to give you that, officer, but in light of all that's happened, I was in a hurry when we left."

The officer sniffed hard, then pointed a few yards down the road.

"Pull over to the side."

"We're not planning on staying, we just need to refuel."

"That wasn't a question. Now pull over," he said in a gruff voice.

"Have we done something wrong, officer?"

"Pull over," he repeated.

Dexter nodded and veered off to the hard shoulder. "Oh great, this is all we need. Deputy Dipshit trying to slow everything down."

"Just stay cool," Aamir said. "They probably just want to make sure we will not cause any trouble. I imagine things have got a little out of control."

Felicity looked in her side mirror at the cop as he made his way over to two other officers and chatted to them. He returned with one officer. One of them looked in the back and eyed them suspiciously. Cops always had a way of making people feel on edge.

"You said you weren't planning on staying."

"No, we're heading for Florida."

His eyes bounced between them. "That's a long way."

"That's why we need gas."

"And you have money?"

Zeke piped up and poked his head between the seats. "I have some."

"Well right now the gas stations are shut down until further notice, so I'm afraid you are out of luck."

"Why would you ask us then?"

He removed his aviator sunglasses and squinted in the late afternoon sun. "Because we've had a lot of trouble over the past forty-eight hours with looters, and people thinking they can just take whatever the hell they like."

"Um officer, you wouldn't happen to have a phone working in town, would you?"

"Unless you know someone or plan on visiting our station, you won't find one in town. It's blocked off to prevent looters from getting at store merchandise."

"Great," Zeke piped up.

The cop eyed him.

"Anyway, unless you are staying the night, I would

recommend you keep on moving. There's nothing here right now that will be of much use. Because of the destruction in the town, I will have to reroute you." He pointed to a road about fifty yards down the road. There was a detour sign set up. "Hang a right and follow that, it will take you around the city and back onto I-40."

"Excuse me, officer," Felicity chimed in. "This is one of the first towns we've come across that doesn't appear to have suffered as much damage. Is the power down?"

"It is, unfortunately."

Dexter gave a nod, and the officer wished them a safe journey and waved them on.

"Well, that's great. Without gas, we aren't going any farther."

Felicity kept staring at the cops in her mirror.

"Just follow the road, the first chance we get we will head into Gallup."

"Are you kidding me? Did you not hear what he said?"

She cut him a glance. "Dexter, we have less than 72 hours to get to Florida otherwise all of us will be dead.

Now I'm not one for going against the law but right now we have no other choice. If they've shut the gas stations, then we need to siphon a couple of vehicles."

"You know this isn't like Flagstaff. If we get caught doing that, they will toss us in a cell and then you can kiss whatever hope of getting home, goodbye."

That was reality. Most of the towns and cities were in ruins but those that had survived would have taken a batten-down-the-hatches approach and declared a state of emergency. Cops would have continued their duties and taken measures to prevent people from stealing gas, food or pharmaceuticals. The majority would set up a council that would address how to ration out food. It would only be a matter of days without communication before lawlessness would rule as people took survival into their own hands. No one would live that long. They were heading south on State Highway 602 before they saw signs for State Highway 564, which would eventually lead them back to I-40. Halfway down 602, Felicity had Dexter veer off onto Old Zuni Road. It fed into a sprawling residential area full of uniform homes.

"You know if we get stopped again, heads will roll," Aamir said. Felicity ignored him, her eyes were scanning the vehicles and homes looking for a place they could park.

"Pull over there," she said.

"I just want to say, I'm against this," Zeke muttered. "If we get caught, I'm denying any involvement."

"That's why you will be the one to get the gas."

"What?" he stammered.

"You're the most able-bodied," Dexter said. "Felicity and Ben have injured themselves, I need to keep an eye on the truck and well, Aamir's not too good at the art of sucking," Dexter said before chuckling.

"Screw you, Dexter."

"I'm just ribbing you, but seriously, get your ass out and siphon a few vehicles."

"We only have one tube."

"Just give it here, I'll do it," Felicity said.

"But..."

"Pass it over," Aamir handed it to her, and she hopped out as soon as he stopped the vehicle. It was still light out and the chances of being spotted were high. Felicity felt like a criminal running at a crouch towards a Chevy truck. She popped the gas cap open and shoved the plastic tubing down the filler tube. It only made it in a few inches before she felt it hit up against something. What the hell? She pulled out the tubing and tried again but still, it wouldn't go.

"You want to tell me what you're doing?" a voice rose from behind her. Her head jerked to the side in time to see a man in his fifties approaching. She quickly pulled the tubing out and backed up.

"No, you stay right here."

Felicity turned to run but a dark mass off to her left plowed into her and pinned her against a car.

"I got her, Dad."

"Get off," she yelled, fighting his son's heavy grasp.

Right then Dexter came running over holding out the Desert Eagle. "I would advise you to listen to her. Now let her go."

The guy immediately backed off with his hands up. "We don't want no trouble."

Felicity motioned to Dexter to head back to the truck. He remained there for a few seconds more before he backed up keeping his weapon trained on them. As soon as she was back in the truck and they tore out of there, the questions started.

"What happened?"

"The damn thing wouldn't go in."

"Are you sure you did it right?" Zeke asked.

"How the hell should I know? I did what Ben was doing back at the last dealership."

"Did you feel something hit the tubing?"

"Yeah."

"It's a ball. An anti-siphon, most new vehicles have them. Basically, there is a ball that is inserted into the filler neck. It prevents people from siphoning. The only way you can get past that is to remove the gas tank or make a hole in it."

"Why didn't you tell her that?"

"I thought she knew."

She exhaled hard. "That guy scared the shit out of me."

"Look, we need to find an older vehicle."

Finding an older vehicle wasn't hard, finding one easy to siphon without going through a repeat of the last scare was making it difficult. It didn't take long to burn through what was left in their own fuel tank. It had already been on low when they entered Gallup. The engine chugged. "Oh man, come on!"

"Over there," Ben said. "Just stop the damn truck, I'll go do it."

"Take the gun," Dexter said handing it off to him.

"I'll go with him," Aamir mumbled.

"Make it fast."

"I'm sorry," Felicity piped up.

"About what?"

"Putting you in that situation."

"Don't worry about it, chances are it won't be the last

time we encounter something like that," Dexter said as they watched Ben and Aamir double-time it up the road towards an older vehicle.

* * *

Ben hurried and flipped open the gas cap and jammed the tube in while Aamir carried the metal canister they'd taken from the dealership. Within a matter of a minute, he was drawing out gasoline and filling up the canister.

"Anyone coming?"

"Nope," Aamir said scanning the houses.

"Come on!" Ben said getting frustrated as the gasoline trickled out. He tried again, and it flowed.

"Do you think we will survive?" Aamir muttered.

"What?" Ben asked barely catching what he said. He was too focused on the task at hand.

"I mean, we are going through all this trouble, for what? Is life going to be any better? We are placing our trust in a government that hasn't even alerted the public to what is coming. So tell me, how can that be any better? What happens if we get all the way to Florida and they decide that we can't go with them?"

"That's not going to happen."

"Why isn't it? Her father doesn't know us. The government sure as hell doesn't owe us anything. And it's not like either of us offer anything in the way of expertise. So why would they allow us on?"

Ben looked up at him and stopped siphoning. "We can't think that way."

"Maybe not but we need to know, don't you think? For all we know she could be lying, just to get us to take her there."

"She wouldn't do that."

"No?"

Ben gazed back down at the gasoline. "The next time she gets on the phone, I'll ask to speak to her father."

"And what if he says he doesn't know? You still want to travel all the way there?"

Ben shrugged. "Look, I know little of anything right now, Aamir. I'm just trying to survive the next ten minutes, never mind what will or won't happen in the distant future."

He returned to siphoning, and once it was done, he screwed the cap back on and they lugged the gas back to the truck and filled it up. When they got in, he cast a glance at Felicity.

"All good?" Felicity asked. Ben nodded and looked at Aamir.

"Yeah."

"Okay, let's get the hell out of here."

No sooner had they pulled out and made it to the far end of the street than two cop cars came screeching ahead of them blocking them in. A cop pushed out of one vehicle and pulled his weapon.

The cop gave a loud command. "Driver. Turn off the engine and step out of the truck."

"Are you kidding? Did someone see you?" Dexter asked eyeing the officers.

"No. I don't think so."

"Then how the hell?"

"The other men, maybe they… Oh God, it doesn't

matter."

"You want me to back up?" Dexter said.

"No. I don't want to end up getting shot," Felicity responded. "Turn off the engine."

Dexter turned it off and following the commands of the officer he removed the keys and placed them on the top of the truck with one hand and then got out. The others were told to stay in there while they handled him. They made Dexter turn around and back up towards the sound of their voice before getting on his knees and placing his hands behind his back. While one officer kept his gun trained on them, the other moved in and handcuffed Dexter.

"Well we can kiss that trip to the moon goodbye," Zeke said.

Within ten minutes they were cuffed, shoved into the back of the cruisers and driven back to the station. Along the way, the officer gave them the third degree. He berated them and acted as if the gasoline was his.

"Did you really think you were going to get away with

it? We might be suffering from a breakdown in communication and a lack of power but people's eyes are still working."

"We just needed gas. We would have paid for it."

"What will happen to us, officer?" Zeke asked.

"That's for the judge to decide."

"Judge? Are you joking?"

The officer glared at him in the rearview mirror — that answered that.

"Look, officer, this has all been a big mistake. We don't have time for this."

"That's what they all say."

"No, I'm dead serious," Zeke said before he blurted it out. "There is an asteroid heading for earth. In less than 72 hours, everything you know is going to be wiped out. It will make these meteorites look like child's play."

"Zeke," Felicity said, shaking her head. She wished he had said nothing. Of course she didn't think anyone would believe them but the last thing they needed was to have the cops peppering her with questions about some government evacuation that she wasn't even sure about herself. She was going on the words of her father, and for all she knew, he was just saying it to get her back so he wouldn't die alone.

"Asteroid? That's original."

"Look around you, deputy, you think this was some small disaster? This is just the precursor to a bigger event. One that is going to wipe out civilization as we know it. Now if you don't let us out..."

"Well hold on a second. If we are all going to die, then why do you want to go? You will not escape it either."

"Oh but that's where you would be wrong. My friend's father works for NASA."

Felicity was quick to interject. "Actually that's not entirely true. He — "

Before she could finish Zeke talked over her. "The government plans to take 100,000 people off this planet before it hits."

Chapter 24

The cops weren't buying any of it. In fact, the officer driving spent the rest of the journey to the department trying not to laugh. He and his partner recounted all the crazy things that people had said to avoid being charged.

Felicity glared at Zeke. "What? It's true."

Aamir who was stuck between them and hadn't said a word since the cops had stuffed them in the back of the cruiser. He looked embarrassed by the whole ordeal.

"You and I are going to have words."

Zeke shook his head and returned to gazing out the window.

The further they went into the heart of the town, the more devastation they could see. At first, it looked as if the town had fared well but that was just the west side, the east was an absolute mess. Homes were torn apart, concrete and twisted metal blocked roads and overpasses had collapsed. Some homes looked as if they belonged to the wealthy, but most of the neighborhoods were working class. From modest homes to brick ranches and shoddy trailers, it was a minefield of devastation. The vehicle rolled past several groups of people outside trying to clear up and restore some semblance of order to their homes. They were oblivious to the threat breathing down earth's neck.

Apart from a few gas stations that were shut down and guarded by cops, there was a school laying in ruins and a fire department that was still standing but had a huge crack down the wall. None of the businesses still standing were in operation.

The City of Gallup Police Department was on 451 Boardman Drive, just at the corner of Boyd Avenue. It was a low-slung, tan-colored structure with a large lot, and multiple cop cars parked outside.

"So you boys have just been tackling this like any other ordinary day," Zeke said trying to connect with them but they weren't having it. The cop riding shotgun cast a glance back and then continued looking ahead without saying a word.

Once parked, the cops hauled them out of the vehicle. Ben and Dexter were in the second cop car that had been following. The two cops watching over them didn't wait for the others, they frog-marched them into the station. Inside it was a chaotic scene. Uniformed officers, along with suits hurried around. They'd set up what looked like a command center with a large map of the town on the wall and several people were talking about what was being done, and shift rotation, while others dealt with unruly locals.

A sergeant was on a landline phone.

"You're in communication with the outside?" Aamir asked.

Neither officer replied.

There were lights on inside the station, no doubt powered by a generator.

On one hand, it was strange to see them going about business as usual but then again it made perfect sense. Emergency services would have already been operating at the time of the meteor shower and earthquakes. As hard as it would have been to continue, they would have seen it as their job to spearhead an operation to maintain order in the town.

However, not everything was running as usual. With so much on their plate, and all their resources being pushed to the limit, anyone causing trouble was led down to the cells.

No paperwork was done, no fingerprints were taken.

"Don't I get a lawyer?" Zeke asked.

"All in good time."

"At least a phone call?" he continued as the officer led them down a series of steps, along a corridor into an area where there were seven cells. One officer watched over them as another unlocked the door and guided them inside. There were already two other people inside a small ten-by-ten room. Ben and Dexter were guided into the room next to theirs. Ben was cursing and bellyaching about how they were just trying to get enough gas to get to the next town. Like that would help. Didn't he understand the first rule of getting arrested? Never admit guilt even if caught red-handed.

"Are you kidding me?" Zeke said. "I'm not sharing a room with a bunch of criminals."

The two individuals glared at him. Aamir slumped down on the floor resigning to the situation that couldn't get much worse.

"I'm sure you'll become acquainted."

"Don't you have a VIP room?"

"Oh yeah, let me go get the keys to that," the officer said shaking his head and locking the door behind him. He pulled down a metal flap and continued to speak.

"Right now we have several pressing matters. An officer will be along shortly to process you all. Have a good day."

With that said, he slammed the shutter and Zeke shouldered the door a few times and yelled. "Hey! I have rights, you know. Do you even know who I am? My lawyers will eat you for lunch. I want your name and badge number."

"Oh, Zeke," Felicity said tapping him. He ignored her for a second and then finally twisted around.

"What?"

She pointed to the two muscle heads who were now heading his way.

"Oh hey guys, you know I was just kidding." He paused and grinned. "Do you want to see a magic trick?"

Chapter 25

The next hour was spent in silence. As the minutes ticked over, what little hope Felicity had of escaping faded. All she could think about was her father going out of his mind with worry. Aamir sat with his back to the wall and with his eyes closed, he was muttering something under his breath. Zeke had paced back-and-forth bellowing to be heard and even earned the respect of two Neanderthals who were inside for trying to loot a store. One of them had seen him on TV and he was curious about how some of the magic was done. With nothing left to lose, Zeke told him.

Rico, the bald-headed Mexican with a tattoo of a dragon down the side of his neck shook his head in complete surprise. "Why didn't I think about that?"

His buddy Carlos laughed and slapped him on the back. "I told you it was all gimmicks."

"So it's just a strong piece of metal that bends and

makes you look like you're levitating?"

"Yep!" Zeke said. "I'm surprised no one ever noticed. I mean even though my pants covered up that leg, it seems obvious."

"And what about levitating in the air?"

"Wires, helicopter and camera tricks. We also would have paid actors."

"Ah man, that sucks. And all along I thought you had special powers."

Zeke laughed. "It's entertainment, my friend, pure illusion. You look this way while I go that way."

"So the whole walking through a window?"

"A trick."

"Damn, I was hoping you could walk through this door and get us out."

They all laughed and then their smiles faded. Felicity was curious to know what had occurred in the town.

"Rico. Where were you when the meteor shower hit?"

"With my kid. Yeah, I was picking him up from school."

"You have a kid?" Zeke said, acting surprised.

"Sure, six to be exact."

"So you and your ex take turns helping each other out?"

"Ex? I'm a married man. I've been married for fourteen years."

"You're joking."

Rico tapped Carlos. "Another one making assumptions. Let me guess, it's the tattoos?"

"No, I've got my own," Zeke said pulling up his sleeve and showing them. "I got this one done by Kat Von D."

"Oh sweet. Damn, now that is a woman I would nail in a heartbeat. Hot as fuck!" Carlos said.

"That she is," Zeke said. "And a fine tattoo artist."

Felicity watched with amused interest as they pored over each other's tattoos and discussed their meaning. "So Rico, did the power go out immediately?"

"Not on the first quake. It was the third one that did it."

"Third?"

They'd only experienced two, which meant there must have been another while they were inside the elevator back at the Luxor.

"Yeah, people panicked. I mean I have kids to feed and the first place everyone went to was the grocery store. The shelves were nearly bare, then people fought over what was left. I literally saw two men beat the shit out of each other over a loaf of bread. That's when I knew things were bad. Anyway, I figured I'd visit one of the convenience stores they had locked up. Break in and gather a few things and then head out of town but we got caught while we were still inside. The owner pulled a gun on us. Kept us there until the cops showed up."

"So the landlines were still working."

"Yeah, as far as I know. Odd, huh?"

"Nah, they usually require a small voltage that gets sent through the line by the telephone and power company. Their backup generators will last for about a week and then they'll stop working."

"But my cell stopped."

"That's usually the first thing to go as it relies on towers," Felicity said. "We learned all this back in Vegas when we were trying to get out."

"What's it like there?"

"A hundred times worse than it is here. You all seemed to have fared well."

He snorted. "That's a good thing, right?"

Frustration kicked in again, and Zeke was up on his feet banging on the door. "Come on, man, we at least should get a phone call."

"Zeke, you are wasting your breath. They haven't been in to see us except to give us food since we got here."

"Which was?"

"A day ago." Rico shook his head. "My wife is probably going out of her mind with worry. She's pregnant. Probably thinks I'm dead."

"This is a human rights violation," Zeke muttered, before slumping back down on the floor. Rico went quiet and shuffled back in the corner of the room. Though he'd been talkative when they arrived, just the mention of his wife had him looking forlorn. There was silence for a while, then Zeke spoke up.

"I've been such a fool. Spent all my time on my work and for what?" He moved his foot back and forth against the hard concrete floor. "My kids don't even know me. I've not been able to hold down a relationship. Hell, if I died tomorrow, no one would show up for my funeral."

"What about family?" Felicity asked. "You must have a family, right? Brothers, sisters?"

"My father died when I was young. I have no siblings and my mother passed away last year."

He cast his eyes to one side.

"Is that why you turned to drinking and drugs?" Felicity asked.

He met her gaze. "It would make sense, right? But no, I was hooked on that long before I lost her." He squeezed his eyes shut and looked as if he was in pain. "No one understands. I felt like a machine, showing up every day and doing those performances. One day just blurred into the next. I was taking uppers to keep me awake, downers to make me relaxed. Throw in a stripper to keep me company and a bottle of Jack Daniel's, and I got lost in it." He stared at her. "You must think I'm a real narcissist, don't you? A sonofabitch that doesn't care for his family or anyone else."

Felicity didn't say a word.

"You would be right. It's not like I woke up like this and to be honest, I'm not sure at what point I stopped caring but I did. Give, give, give, sign this, attend that show, make sure you're at this meeting, do this performance. There's only so much of that you can do before you start to…" he tapped his temple. "Lose your mind." He breathed out hard. "I care. I care about my kids. I care about what people think of me. I'm just not very good at…"

"Saying and doing the right things?" she asked, finishing what she assumed he was about to say. He nodded.

"Join the club. We've all got baggage."

Zeke stared up at the ceiling and drummed his fingers

on the floor.

"We're not going to get out of here, are we?"

"We are."

Felicity rose to her feet and crossed the room to the door. She banged a few times. Minutes passed, then an hour before an officer showed up. The steel flap on the door clanged as he opened it.

"Keep it down."

"Listen, I want to make one phone call. I'm entitled to that."

It wasn't the same officer as the one that had put them in. He was a younger guy, with a mustache and dark eyes. "Who are you going to call?"

"My father."

"Oh, the one who's planning to..." He made a gesture to space. "Yeah, I heard about that. That gave the guys upstairs a good laugh."

"Look, I don't care what you think. I'm entitled to a phone call."

"Give her the call, man!" Rico shouted.

"Yeah," Carlos added.

The cop looked off to his right. "All right. But one call and that's it."

He took out his keys and unlocked the door. Zeke got up to leave and was pushed back in. "Not you. Just her."

"Oh come on, I have rights too."

"That you do, and we have procedure. Take a seat."

Zeke huffed and went over to the far side of the room. The officer locked the door back up and led her along the corridor and up the stairs.

"I really appreciate this, Officer…" she said, feeling the first sliver of hope since they'd arrived. If anyone could get them out of this mess, it was her father. At the bare minimum, at least she could tell him where she was.

"Moody," the officer replied.

He guided her to a desk in a small corner office and slid a landline phone in front of her. "Two minutes, that's it." After saying that, he closed the door behind him, and took a seat across from her. She studied him for a second and looked out of the office window. He must have noticed as he got up and closed the blinds. To say his actions were a little odd would have been an understatement. Felicity fished into her pocket for the number her father gave her before picking up the phone. The number she was dialing would connect her with a satellite phone. Unlike cell phones, which relied on land-based towers, he was using a government phone that communicated directly with a satellite orbiting the earth. It was helpful for communicating over a much wider area and was often used by the military. It sent a signal to the satellite and then back to the nearest land-based station or teleport. It could communicate with landlines, which made it ideal for the shitty situation she found herself in.

"You going to listen in?"

"Yep," he replied, before giving a wry smile.

Felicity brought a hand up to her face and turned slightly, trying to get privacy, not that it would help as he leaned forward, curious to hear what she was about to say.

Chapter 26

The phone rang several times before her father picked up. When he answered he sounded both elated and worried to hear from her.

"Oh God, Felicity, why has it taken you so long to call?"

"Besides the fact that the entire planet has suffered a major setback, well, let me see…" She rattled off what had occurred until the point of their arrest.

"Arrested?"

"Look, don't worry about that. Just tell me you're sending a helicopter to pick us up."

"It's not looking good here, Felicity."

She leaned back in her seat and put a hand to her forehead. "And you think it's any better here?"

"I know, it's just hard trying to get anyone to see sense."

"Meaning, they no longer want to risk it?"

He was quiet on the other end.

"Just say it, Dad, no one is coming."

"No, it's just if you had been closer we might have."

"Dad, listen." She glanced up at a clock on the wall and did the math in her head as to when they left Henderson, how long they'd been on the road and how much time they had wasted inside police custody. "The chances of us making it back in time are slim to none. They will not let us out of here, not after what's happened."

"Tell them what is about to happen."

"We already have!" she said, her voice getting louder. Officer Moody leaned forward trying to eavesdrop. Felicity cupped a hand over the receiver, lowered her voice and turned her back to him. She leaned forward. "They don't believe us."

"Then let me speak to them."

"You're not understanding, Dad. It doesn't matter whether they believe you or not, in their eyes, we have committed a criminal act and they are treating it like they would any other crime. Besides, think about what they are going to say if you tell them you need us home because we have a flight to catch."

He went quiet.

"Your two minutes are up."

Felicity turned. "Please just give me another minute."

The officer narrowed his eyes and cast a glance at his watch. "Fine, but make it quick."

She gave a strained smile as the reality of her situation closed in on her.

"Felicity, give the phone to the officer."

"But—"

"Felicity!"

She clenched her jaw. She hadn't heard her father shout in a long time and the last time it had happened she walked out on him and moved to Vegas. She held out the phone without looking at the officer. "He wants to speak to you."

"To me?"

She gave a nod, and the officer took it.

"Officer Moody, how can I help?"

There was a long period of silence before the officer replied.

"Uh-huh. Yes. No." He laughed. "Are you serious?"

Again more silence, except now his features had hardened, and a look of great concern appeared on his face. "And you can prove this, how?"

He held the phone in the crook of his neck and turned to Felicity. "Seems you might not be full of shit."

Someone else must have come on the line as he mentioned the name William.

"My wife, mother and two brothers."

Felicity frowned as she tried to make sense of the conversation.

"Possibly. And you can guarantee that?"

He eyed her and got this faint smile on his face.

"You know what you're asking me to do?"

The officer perched on the edge of the table, then he looked at his watch.

"In four hours? Yeah. Hold on a second, let me give

you the coordinates."

The officer placed the phone down and went over to a computer and powered it up. Felicity made a gesture to see if it was okay for her to speak with her father again and the cop waved her on.

"Dad. What is going on?"

"I'm coming to get you. The officer will bring you out."

"How? How did you arrange that?"

"How do you think? I promised him a one-way ticket along with his family."

"Right. So them and my friends?"

There was a long pause.

"Dad?"

"Yeah, I was meaning to speak to you about that. I… um, I spoke with the powers that be and unfortunately, there isn't room for them."

"But there is room for this cop and his family?"

"Felicity, you need to understand. My priority is getting you to safety. Not ensuring the safety of anyone else."

"The only reason I'm still alive, Dad, is because of them."

"I'm sorry, Felicity, it's not my call."

"And yet you can promise a cop and his family a seat? Sounds like you have enough seats, it's just they have nothing to offer."

"No, it's not that. Well. I mean, the list is compiled of those who will be of use."

"Of use? So you are saying if people don't hold a high and lofty position in society, they don't get on it? Well what about me? Do you even know what I have been doing for the past two years? Huh? Let me tell you. I've been selling my body. That's right. Your little girl has been sleeping with men for money, just to make ends meet."

"But…" He went to say something and then remained quiet.

"So if they are only taking those who are of use," she emphasized the word *use*. "Then I guess I shouldn't be on that list either unless they need someone to sleep with government officials."

"Don't be like that."

"You know what, Dad, I would take these four guys over any number of military and cops you can stuff in that airship."

"You have to understand, Felicity, there is room, but it's limited. Hell, I don't get to make the choices. If it weren't for William, I wouldn't even be on that list. But. Well. The situation has changed and now I must do what is best for you."

"Are you sure it's for me and not you?"

"Look, I'm not doing this now."

She gritted her teeth and could feel her temperature rising.

"You know that this is out of my hands. I have already had William go to bat for you several times and he risked his career because of it. So don't even go there."

"Oh, I guess I should be thankful then. Is that what you are saying?"

"Oh come on, Felicity, don't be so facetious. I don't want to fight. Please. I'm doing the best I can under these conditions and we are running out of time. Now I still have to arrange for a pilot to take me out to where you are. It will take four hours to get there, then another four to get back. We are down to the wire here. Just put the cop back on."

She handed the phone off to him and he smiled and shook his head as he took it. He gave him the directions to Fort Wingate Army Depot, which was an abandoned depot located seven miles east of Gallup. As she listened in, he mentioned it was a twenty-minute drive. He nodded a few times, then said one last thing which sounded like a threat.

"If you are lying, it won't end well."

As soon as he got off the phone, he leaned back in the chair and put his arms behind his head as if he'd just sealed the deal of the century. In some ways he had.

"Well, I'm going to get my family, and then I'll return and we'll take a little trip out to Fort Wingate. Your old man better be on the up and up, otherwise…" he trailed off as he knew she had already heard his conversation. She glanced up at the clock and made a mental note of when he would arrive. It would be dark out.

Chapter 27

As Officer Moody took the keys out to unlock her cell, she spoke up, "Do you think I could have my two other friends in the cell with us? You know, so I can see them before we leave."

He stared at her, his hand still holding the key in the lock. Then he shrugged. "Darlin', you can have anything you like because four hours from now, I'm going to be on a Black Hawk heading to safety, all thanks to your old man." He removed the key and went over to the cell that had Dexter and Ben inside and unlocked it.

"Okay, guys, out you come, you're going in the next cell."

"What?" Dexter said, hopping up from the bed. "I thought you were releasing us."

"Not today."

They walked out past Felicity and she dropped her chin. She wanted to be the one to tell them. After all they'd done for her, she thought they deserved to know. Moody transferred them into the next cell but before Felicity entered, he pulled her to one side. "What you told your father, about what you did for a living, was that for real?"

She eyed him but never replied and stepped inside.

"I'll be back soon. Sit tight."

The door clunked behind her, letting out a deafening echo, and she exhaled hard.

Dexter flung his hands up. "Okay, you want to tell me why you requested that we join you in here?" he asked. "Cause, while I don't like being in this place, being stuck in here with Zekey boy and the two amigos is definitely not making it any better."

"I…"

"Felicity?" Ben asked. "What is it?"

How could she begin to tell them? There was no easy way to drop it on them. No matter how she tried to sugar coat it, it wasn't going down well. She leaned back against a wall for support.

Aamir got up from the floor. "Did you speak with your father?"

She nodded.

"And? Is he coming?"

Again she nodded but they could tell something was wrong.

"What are you not telling us?"

"My father made a deal with Officer Moody to ensure that I'm on that helicopter."

"Fantastic!" Zeke said smashing a fist into his open hand. "Finally we can get the hell out of here."

"To ensure *I'm* on there," she repeated, placing emphasis to make it clear. Zeke's smile faded.

"Right, you, us."

She shook her head.

"I told you," Aamir said. "It was never going to be us." He turned and walked back to his place against the wall and slumped down.

"No, that's not true. I made arrangements with him to make sure that all of you would board that helicopter. It's just…"

"Just what, Felicity? Spit it out."

"There's no easy way to say this. The cops aren't going to let us out, so he made a deal with him to release me in exchange for letting the officer and his family on board the helicopter."

"Okay?" Dexter said shaking his head. "Black Hawks can carry at least eleven people. So?"

"It's not your seat on the Black Hawk that isn't available, it's the one on the *Deliverance.* By making the deal, it means he can no longer offer it to you four."

Dexter's jaw dropped. Ben squeezed the bridge of his nose as if a tension headache was coming on, and Zeke let out a chuckle. "Ain't that just beautiful. Oh, the irony." He reached into his pocket and pulled out a scrap of paper with the address of his kid in Florida. Shaking his head, he crumpled it up and pushed it back in and turned away. Rico and Carlos looked on a little confused.

"You want to bring me up to speed on what the hell you all are going on about?" Rico asked. Zeke laughed, almost doubling over.

"You wouldn't believe me if I told you," Zeke said.

"Try me," he replied.

Over the course of the next five minutes, Zeke brought them up to speed on the events that had transpired, and her father's position and the life-saving opportunity they had before them until they were arrested.

"Shit. I thought we had it bad," Carlos said. "Your lives are seriously fucked up, homies."

"That they are, Carlos, that they are," Zeke said before taking a seat on the steel toilet.

Few words were exchanged after that. It would only be a matter of time before Officer Moody returned and then that would be the last time she'd ever see them. Time seemed to move slowly. Aamir got up and stretched out his back, Zeke continued to share every single one of his magic secrets with Rico, and Dexter laid on the hard cot, arms behind his head and eyes closed. Ben was the only one that hadn't taken his eyes off Felicity. After a while, she got a complex.

"What is it, Ben? Spit it out. You've been staring at me for the last hour."

He seemed hesitant but then he spoke. "So you're giving up?"

"It's over, Ben."

"We've traveled almost five hundred miles and faced numerous obstacles and not once did I hear you say it's over."

"There's nothing more we can do."

"If I believed that, I would have given up when I was sandwiched between two pieces of concrete."

"Well, theoretically, you weren't actually pinned down by the concrete. Your clothing was."

"Thanks for the correction, Ahab," Ben said without even looking at him. "What I'm saying is, until that asteroid hits, we still have options."

She shook her head. "No, you don't understand. That cop. He's coming back and he'll take me out of here and leave all of you inside." She paused. "He's not coming back. They are overwhelmed, understaffed and this situation isn't getting any better. Upstairs, I only saw a couple of cops. All the rest are out there, or have left. Probably quit."

"So what? We just stop trying?"

She pushed off from the wall and got close to him. "We can't get out of here. And even if we could, they would be on our ass before we got on that helicopter. Saying we can still do it, isn't going to make it happen."

"Well, then what would make it happen?"

"Killing the cop," Rico said. His eyes flitted over. "You prepared to do that?"

Ben stared at the ground. "Then if that's it, then that's it."

"We're not taking a cop's life."

"Felicity, everyone on this planet will be dead soon. Now you have to decide, what matters to you? Your life or his? And before you say anything, remember we've already had to deal with a situation like this."

He cast a glance at Zeke and Dexter who had taken the lives of the bikers.

"So what's it going to be?"

Her eyes bounced between them.

Chapter 28

It had taken Officer Moody the better part of three hours before Felicity heard the thump of his boots approaching the cell. He was whistling some upbeat tune as if he didn't have a care in the world. The steel flap on the door dropped, and he peered in.

"Miss Meyer, time to go. I hope you've said your goodbyes."

She nodded and rose to her feet, her eyes darting across to the others.

Her pulse beat faster at the clunk of the key being inserted into the lock. Moody pulled back the door and waved her on out while keeping a firm grip on the door handle. "Come on, we don't have long."

She turned to Dexter and gave him a hug, then did the same with Zeke.

"Speed it up, we don't have all day," he said sounding frustrated.

When she continued with Aamir, followed by Ben, Moody stepped inside.

"Okay, that's enough, we have to—"

Before he'd even finished his words, Carlos attacked him, dragging him down to the cell floor and pinning him against the ground before he went for his handgun.

"Don't kill him," Felicity said as she looked back at the cell door to see if anyone was coming. "Just cuff and gag him."

As he did that, Dexter reached down and took the weapon from his holster.

"You're making a big mistake. You won't get out of here."

"Oh, you'd be surprised at what we can get out of," Dexter said, patting the side of his face and then fishing into his pockets for a key fob to his cruiser. Rico reached across and pulled the extendable baton from his duty belt and gave it a sharp jerk to produce the metal rod that shot out. Not wasting any time, they streamed out of the cell and slid along the corridor with their backs against the wall.

"Now that's what I call some serious misdirection, hey Zekey boy?"

Both of them smiled, just glad to be free of the cell. Rico slammed the door closed on the cell and locked it but not before giving Moody a few sharp kicks to the gut.

"You're lucky that girl doesn't want you dead, otherwise I would have taken great joy in beating you to death."

"Rico," Felicity shouted to him.

Felicity stared up at the camera in the corner of the long stretch of corridor. Was anyone seeing this play out? Was anyone even upstairs? She recalled only seeing two cops in the main building when she phoned her father. With the generator fired up and power keeping all their equipment running, she figured they'd soon find out. She put a hand up as they waited by the staircase that led up to the main floor and listened for anyone coming.

There was nothing.

As Dexter was armed, he led the way.

"I still think we should have killed him," Carlos said.

"He was just doing his job," she replied.

"Does his job involve making a deal for his own family? The guy was about to go AWOL," Zeke said. "I don't see any honor in that. In fact, it makes you wonder if he's told anyone."

"And risk his own seat on that Hawk? Why would he?" Ben said.

When they made it to the top of the stairs, Dexter looked from side to side before waving them on. They headed for an exit at the far end.

"You know his family is outside waiting for him."

"It doesn't matter."

Right then, just as Dexter said that a cop stepped out from a doorway holding paperwork in his hand. His eyes were down. All of them froze, and for a brief second time seemed to slow as the cop looked their way then....

"Don't do it!" Dexter yelled as the cop dropped the paperwork and went for his gun.

A single shot echoed, and the cop bounced off the wall

and crumpled.

There was no time for the shock to set in. All of them sprinted towards the exit, realizing that firing that round was like setting off a warning alarm. As they hurried past what had originally been the central command center, Carlos scooped up the dead cop's gun and opened fire on two more cops who had taken cover behind desks. One of them squeezed off a round, and it struck Carlos in the leg bringing him to the floor. He returned fire and killed another cop.

Had this been any other day, under any other conditions, their chances of making it outside in one piece would have been slim to none, but because every cop and all the resources they had were out on the streets assisting the public and preventing people from stealing gasoline and supplies, the station was practically deserted, running with nothing more than a skeleton crew.

Felicity's nerves were fried as she pressed on towards the exit, just trying to make it out of there alive. Rico raced into the command center, gripping a baton and vaulting over a desk as the other officer shot at him. "Motherfuck—"

She didn't slow down to see what happened to him, but she heard the crunch of metal hitting something hard.

Dexter burst through the exit door and scanned the area for threats. It led out to a parking lot at the side of the building. He immediately pressed the button on the key fob and waited to hear the sound and the flash of lights on a cruiser. What he got instead was a black SUV that already had people inside — Moody's family.

With his gun at the ready, Dexter raced towards the vehicle yelling for them to get out. The doors opened and two women rolled out, their hands shot up begging him to not shoot. On the far side of the vehicle two men jumped out and in the chaos of the moment a gun went off. Dexter reacted the only way he would when coming under fire, he returned fire, unloading two rounds into one man's chest. A flash of motion from off to the side and the other guy dropped to his knees laying down a rifle. Dexter lowered his weapon when he saw it was just a teenager.

"Felicity!"

She wheeled around to find Aamir holding Zeke. He was clutching his stomach. The round had hit him. "Oh my God," she cried as she hurried back and dropped beside him.

"Ain't it just my luck," he said trying to crack a smile.

"Don't speak. Aamir, help me get him in the vehicle."

They raised him up with his arms around them and hurried him over to the waiting vehicle. Dexter was already in the SUV and had started it up. It rumbled to life, and they slipped into the back before he gunned the motor and fishtailed out of the lot, leaving behind a plume of dust and Moody's family weeping over the fallen.

Dexter flipped on the main beams and lit up the road ahead. Zeke was in a bad state, blood was gushing out of his stomach and he was fading in and out of consciousness.

"Zeke, stay with me, buddy. Don't go to sleep," Aamir

said. Felicity had torn off her shirt and was holding it against the wound to slow the bleeding but it wasn't helping. There was too much blood.

"Felicity," Zeke mumbled.

"Don't speak," she said, her eyes welling up. Zeke fished into his pocket and produced the crumpled piece of paper. He handed it to her, covered in bloodstains.

"It's the address of my kid in Florida." He coughed hard, and blood trickled out the side of his mouth. "If there is time, please, please check on him. Have him take my spot."

"Take your spot? No, you're gonna be okay," she said, trying to stay optimistic in a situation slipping out of her grasp.

He shook his head and smiled. "Dexter, you make damn sure she gets on that helicopter."

Dexter flashed a look in the mirror as he swerved onto a dusty road that led out of the city. He nodded but didn't reply. "After all we've been through, I can't have you fucking this up." He laughed, and more blood came out of his mouth and he winced in pain.

"Promise me," he said, gripping her hand. "Promise you will check in on him. His name is Adam."

She took the paper from his hand and with a few tears streaming down her face she nodded. "You have my word."

His eyelids closed, and he coughed a few more times.

"Dexter, can you go any faster?" Ben asked.

"I'm giving it everything it has."

They tore out of the city heading east on I-40, following the signs for Fort Wingate. Based on how many miles were displayed on the sign, they figured it would take close to twenty minutes. It was pitch dark on the road, and Dexter had to keep adjusting, slowing down and weaving his way around obstacles. Though the fear of crashing into a crevice was at the forefront of everyone's mind, it wasn't what bothered her the most. Zeke had gone a pale white, and Felicity knew he wasn't going to make it. He'd already lost too much blood.

"How long until your father gets here?" Dexter yelled.

"Aamir, your watch. What time is it?"

"Just after nine twenty."

Three hours had already passed since she'd last spoken with her father. It would take them another twenty minutes to reach the army depot, and then it would be a waiting game.

"He didn't give an exact time. He said it would take four hours. Whether he secures a Black Hawk, and whether or not he leaves on time is anyone's guess."

"Well, I hope he gets his ass here soon because once they let Moody out of that cell, and he finds out we just killed one of his family members, he's going to be one pissed-off dude, and he knows where we are heading."

The reality of what he said, hit all of them hard.

While she didn't imagine he would rally up a crew of officers to head out of town, it remained a real threat. Felicity turned back to Zeke who was hanging on by a thread. His eyelids would open, and close, and his breathing had become shallow.

She gripped his hand, wanting to make sure he knew

in his final moments he wasn't alone. No matter how he had lived his life, the mistakes he'd made, the frustration he'd caused, she knew behind the walls he'd put up to keep people at a distance, he had a good heart.

Eventually, she felt the strength in his hand go weak and he breathed his last breath.

No one could have prepared her for that moment.

In the short time, she'd known him, he'd become like family. It might have sounded odd to anyone else, but that's what it felt like to her. He wasn't some great celebrity, as he was perceived in life, he wasn't just a rich asshole who had more money than sense, he was a human being that had stuck with them through the worst situations. Some might have said he only stayed with them because he feared for his own life, but she knew that wasn't true. Felicity gazed down at the crumpled piece of paper. He had the hope of seeing his kid again, and maybe, just maybe starting a different life beyond the earth.

She muttered a quiet prayer over him, then looked out

the window into the blackness.

Dad, I hope you get here soon.

Chapter 29

The atmosphere inside the SUV was somber as they made their way along the final stretch, turning south off I-40. Upon arrival at Fort Wingate Army Depot, the headlights swept over a field of ordnance bunkers. They were about the same size and shape as Quonset huts and there were hundreds of them.

"What the hell are those?"

Aamir knew. He was like a walking encyclopedia.

"Ordnance bunkers. They were created after World War I and they continued to expand them during World War II and the Korean War. Unfortunately, the place is a ghost town now it has been decommissioned. There have been a lot of disputes between the government and Native Americans over the use of the land and its development. Seems everyone wants a piece of the pie."

"Aamir, how the hell do you know all this?"

"Like I said, I majored in history, I met a lot of

interesting folks driving people around Vegas, and I got a lot of downtime."

"And you spent it studying U.S. history?" Ben muttered.

"You make it sound like a bad thing." He chuckled and for a brief few seconds, their minds were distracted. Dexter hadn't cracked a smile since leaving the police station. When he parked outside the two-story old Fort Wingate barracks, it was shrouded in darkness. Nothing but miles of flat landscape, trees and the red rock mesa in the distance.

They got out and gazed around at the desolate location that had once been home to the military back in the 1900s.

"We should bury him," Aamir said staring at Zeke's lifeless body.

"What? Out here?" Dexter asked. "I didn't know the guy but from what I learned, I think he would roll in his grave if he knew we left him in some ditch in the middle of nowhere."

"So we'll take him," Felicity said.

"Are you serious?" Ben asked. "I mean, I'm all for giving him a proper burial but it's not practical."

"So we bury him."

"Out here?" Dexter said it again as if he gave a damn.

"You fought constantly with him the whole way, why does it matter? He's gone."

"I know but what would he have wanted? What would we have wanted if it was one of us?" Dexter asked. They looked at one another but said nothing. It was an awkward position to find themselves in. "And besides, do you even have a shovel?"

"Good point."

"We'll take him." And that was it. They carried his body off the vehicle and laid him down in preparation to evacuate, then stood around waiting for her father to arrive.

Dexter sat on the hood of the SUV smoking a cigarette from a pack he found in the vehicle. Ben was taking a piss nearby and Aamir was staring up into the sky.

"What if they don't take us?" Aamir asked.

"What?" Felicity asked.

Aamir turned. "I know you said your father would secure a spot for us, but what if that changes once they get here?"

"It won't."

"But if it does?"

"Aamir. If it does, then I don't go."

Dexter chuckled, blowing a plume of smoke. "Yeah like you would do that."

She turned towards him frowning. "You don't know what I would or wouldn't do."

"Whatever, I'm just saying." He leaned back on the hood and continued taking a long drag on his cigarette.

"You know, Dexter, what your problem is?"

"I'm sure you will tell me."

"You think no one gives a shit about you, and so you've lived your life keeping everyone at a distance."

"So have you."

"So has everyone, except Aamir."

He piped up. "Actually that's not true."

They all looked back at him. "My wife and kids, they lived in a separate apartment."

"What?" Ben said focusing his attention back on him while laughing. "Are you telling me, Ahab, you're divorced?"

"Separated, not divorced. We were working through some issues."

"And there was me thinking you were such a big family man." Ben grinned as he made his way back over to the rest of them while doing up his fly. "Tell me something, if you were separated, why did you continue to wear that ring?"

"Because I don't believe in divorce."

"So why did you leave your wife?"

"She left me."

"Why?"

"Over money!" he shouted growing frustrated with this line of questioning.

"Ain't that always the way," Dexter said without even

looking at them.

"I think we are missing the point here," Felicity chimed in. "What I was trying to say is the only reason we are alive is because of each other."

"Yeah," he gave a wink. "I think Zekey boy would disagree."

"You know what I mean."

Dexter tossed up a hand. "Hey, I have no beef with you. Continue on with your grand speech."

She eyed him with a look of disdain and was about to say something when Ben called out, "Hey guys. Guys!"

"What is it?"

"We've got company."

Coming across the desert plain, two sets of headlights cut through the night. They bounced every so often, and a thin plume of dust kicked up behind the vehicles.

"And it looks like they are in a hurry."

"Shit!" Dexter rolled off the hood. "Carlos was right, we should have killed him." Dexter hurried to the back of the SUV and pulled out the rifle they'd taken off the teen and tossed his handgun to Ben. He handed Aamir the second handgun, from the guy who shot Zeke. "Felicity, head into the barracks, and the rest of you fan out. The second you get a chance to take them down, take the shot."

"What about Zeke?" Aamir asked. His words were lost in the sound of everyone hurrying to find cover. Aamir went with Felicity and he handed off the gun to her. "I can't do it. I've shot no one."

She took the handgun from him and they took shelter inside one room on the ground floor of the barracks. All the windows had been smashed out and there was nothing inside except an old metal bed frame. The walls were covered in graffiti and it looked as if someone had started a fire in the corner of the room as the wood was charred.

Felicity saw that Dexter had taken a knee behind a piece of rusted steel nearby, and Ben was behind the vehicle.

Come on, Dad, she muttered under her breath, her eyes

looking up for any sign.

One of the approaching vehicles was a police cruiser, the other an SUV. The cruiser barreled forward doing at least ninety, while the other tried to keep up. As it fishtailed into the property, it turned sideways and though visibility was low, Felicity could see two people inside. A door cracked open on the far side of the vehicle and she could just make out the silhouette of a man crouched down, then another being shoved out into the open.

"Now listen up!" a voice bellowed over a megaphone, from a guy hidden behind the cruiser. His voice was unmistakable. It was Officer Moody. He kept shifting position. They watched in silence as the other individual stumbled forward and then collapsed to his knees a few feet from the car, directly in the path of the headlights. That's when they got their first look at who it was.

Rico.

His head hung low, and his wrists were cuffed.

He also looked like he'd taken one hell of a beating.

The other SUV had several individuals inside. It parked farther back. The driver's door opened, and another officer hurried over to where Moody was.

"I don't blame you for what you did back there. It's to be expected under the circumstances, but killing my brother — that is unforgivable. So I will make this real easy for you. You come on out, put your weapons down and we won't kill your friend here."

Dexter shouted out, laughter mixed with his words. "Are you for real?"

There was no response.

"I'll tell you what, give me a second to think that over, and I'll give you an answer," Dexter replied. She watched as he checked the rifle and then got into a prone position at the corner of his cover.

"What's he doing?" Aamir said, his head bobbing back and forth while squinting.

A single shot resounded and Rico slumped back.

"How's that for an answer? I saved you the trouble."

Felicity stared at Rico in shock and disbelief.

"Holy shit!" Aamir said. "Dexter has gone mad."

"No, Moody has," she said shaking her head. To think he could use someone they didn't even know as a bargaining chip wasn't just foolish, it was insane. Sure, Rico had assisted them in getting out but they didn't know him. What Dexter did may have come across as cold but taking that shot was a no-brainer. He would have probably died in the cross-fire, anyway.

Gunfire began, a chaotic eruption, each one pinging off the metal that Dexter was laying behind. Dexter shifted position, running at a crouch off into the darkness.

"Your brother shot our friend," Ben shouted. "What did you expect us to do?"

Moody's reply was swift, he unleashed a flurry of rounds that peppered the vehicle, some hitting the tires and causing them to deflate, the rest puncturing holes in the body. Ben ducked down, covering his head with his hands. She saw one of the officer's dart out from the cruiser while Moody continued to keep them under fire.

Felicity brought up her handgun and squeezed off a round. She'd held a gun, but it had been up close and she hadn't fired it. Back when she dumped her pimp, she carried a small firearm in her purse after a situation with a rough john had left her out of pocket, and badly bruised.

She squeezed the trigger and two rounds lanced the dusty landscape near the officer's feet causing him to rush back for cover. Now their attention was focused on her. She fired a few more rounds at the cruiser before ducking down and telling Aamir to head out. She knew better than to stay in the same spot.

The sound of gunshots echoed in the night over the next twenty minutes.

"I still can't believe he killed Rico," Aamir said.

She hadn't given it much thought, she was just trying to keep her head down and stay alive. Ben hurried over and slid into the barracks to join them while Dexter continued to keep them under fire and locked down behind the cruiser. The SUV they arrived in was now nothing but a shell. All the windows were shattered, the wheels deflated, and the body looked like Swiss cheese.

"Shit, I'm out," Felicity said tossing the gun down. "What about you?"

Ben pulled out the magazine and looked. "Maybe three rounds left."

Right then a helicopter could be heard approaching. Ben looked at her and his eyes widened. "You think?"

"God, I hope so. Let's go," she said hurrying out of the room and down the corridor out into the night. Almost immediately they came under fire. A bullet struck Felicity in the leg, buckling her knees. She screamed out in pain and hit the ground. Ben returned fire and then scrambled to help her. Panic took hold as she looked down at the wound. It had torn through her lower right thigh. She was clutching it as Aamir tried to create a tourniquet.

"Where are they?" Felicity yelled, her face covered in tears. All she could think about was her father landing in a war zone and getting hit by a stray bullet, or worse, them taking the pilot and her father hostage to get out.

They had nothing to lose. They knew the situation

and would do whatever they could to ensure they were on that helicopter.

"Listen, I need to get over to where Dexter is and help him. Aamir, get her on that helicopter." He nodded. Ben went to rush off and Felicity grabbed him.

"Don't you die on me."

He smiled. "I'm not planning on it."

With that said he rushed off zigzagging his way across the arid desert, shrouded only by a few trees and the darkness of the night. Aamir helped her up, and they stumbled forward toward the Black Hawk which was setting down a hundred yards away.

The rotors were kicking up a wave of dust making visibility bad.

* * *

Dexter was laughing when Ben made it to him. He was ducked down behind an old trailer that had become a part of the landscape. Long weeds and wild grass had grown up around it, smothering every inch.

"God, these assholes are pissing me off."

"It's time to go," he said.

Dexter rolled over and pulled out a cigarette, and lit it.

"We aren't both going to get out, not without cover. You go."

"No, screw your heroics. No one else is dying tonight."

"Ben, I promised that narcissistic asshole I would get her on that Hawk and…"

Ben grabbed him around the collar while keeping an eye on the two officers who appeared to be reloading as they'd stopped firing. "For once, listen to someone. We are not dying out here."

Dexter smiled. "You know, Ben, I've only lived for twenty-four years on this ball of dirt and I've felt more alive in the last two days than before that. Do you think if this shit show hadn't happened and we had met under different circumstances we would have had a beer together?"

"Probably not."

He smirked. "Yeah, I didn't think so either."

He brought up his rifle.

"How many rounds you got?"

"Two," Ben said.

"You will need those to get back to that chopper. Now move your ass. I'll be right behind you."

Ben studied him for a second, then cast a glance towards the Black Hawk that had landed. He patted him on the back. "See you at the chopper."

Gunshots echoed as he dashed at a crouch. His leg was killing him. It had swollen badly over the past twenty-four hours and he was pretty sure the damn thing was infected. As he ran, he turned back and saw Dexter rising and squeezing off rounds while slowly backing up.

* * *

Lieutenant Tom Harley was the first one to reach her, followed by Charlie. Both were geared up ready to engage. Her father wrapped his arms around Felicity and squeezed her tightly while her friend hurried back towards another man hobbling towards them. Harley went to assist.

"God, I thought I had lost you."

They held each other for a few seconds longer before she turned to check on her friends. She staggered a little, and he saw her bloodstained pants. He tried to guide her back to the Hawk, but she refused.

"Felicity."

"I'm not leaving without them."

"Where's the cop?"

"He's not coming. We need to…"

Her words caught in her throat as she saw one of her friends drop.

"Dexter!"

Though her leg was burning, and she was in agony, Felicity pushed the pain from her mind, broke away from him and he grabbed her by the arm.

"No, get in the helicopter, we need to go."

"I'm not leaving without them."

"Harley!" Charlie shouted, motioning to grab his daughter. He turned and scooped her up in one arm while holding his M4 in the other. She kicked and screaming as he hauled her back to the Black Hawk. He'd got within spitting distance from Charlie when she begged them to help the others.

"No time," he muttered. "We need to go."

She wasn't having any of it. Felicity kneed Harley in the nuts and broke away, zigzagging her way across the ground towards her friend.

"Shit!"

* * *

Felicity felt like she was running for a touchdown. Each step was more agonizing than the last. She stumbled several times and hit the ground, but got up again. Rounds continued to fire, some zipped past her as she raced past Aamir and Ben and made her way over to Dexter. He was lying on the ground, continuing to return fire but had taken a shot to the shoulder, and one to the leg.

He grimaced rolling around in agony. "What the hell are you doing here?" he asked.

"I'm not leaving without you."

"You're injured," he spat out.

"So are you."

"Get your ass on that Hawk."

"Shut the hell up and let someone help you for once."

"God, you are as stubborn as the rest of them."

"Get used to it, you're stuck with us," she said.

She grabbed the rifle out of his hands and took over firing at the officers trying to move towards them but weren't making much ground. From behind her, she heard boots approaching and turned to find Ben, Aamir, and the military guy. They scooped up Dexter and carried him away while the military guy ordered her to get into the helicopter or he would shoot her himself. Felicity backed off while he covered her.

Two minutes later, she joined the others. Onboard the pilot was treating Dexter's wounds. Her father snagged up a rifle and assisted the man who they came to learn was a lieutenant.

As soon as he had his ass in that Hawk, it lifted leaving behind the two officers and their family. Would they have attacked under any other conditions? Probably not. They were desperate like thousands of others out there. Self-preservation could motivate anyone to kill.

"So this is your daughter," Harley said, his stern eyes bouncing from her father to her.

"That she is," he said wrapping his arm around her and squeezing her tight.

"Tough girl," he said before his lip curled up and he returned to looking out.

She cast a glance at Ben, Dexter, and Aamir who looked exhausted. Ben offered back a smile before clasping Dexter's hand. She looked back towards where they came from, pain coursing through her body, her heart heavy from losing Zeke. She fished into her pocket and handed the paper to her father.

"Before we leave, I need someone to check this address."

"I hope you are joking," Lieutenant Harley said.

She shook her head.

"Who's it for?" Charlie asked.

She looked back towards the army depot as it blurred

into the darkness.

"A friend."

Epilogue

Five Months Later

The young boy stood in one of the observation stations gazing out at the earth that was hidden behind a cloud of dust. Felicity walked up beside him and he cast a glance before looking down again on a world that was no longer inhabitable. It would take years before they could venture down and see what had become of it. In the meantime, thousands of people were adapting to life on the *Deliverance*, trying to carve out an existence.

"Quite a sight, isn't it?" Felicity asked.

He breathed in. "Do you think we will ever return?" Adam asked.

"If we do, life won't be the same."

He nodded and there was a long pause as they soaked in the sight of the world they'd left behind. It seemed surreal to be looking down on a planet that had once held over 7 billion lives. Now all that remained was 100,000. Though life was different now, some things remained the same. Everyone continued to contribute in meaningful ways. Felicity worked alongside her father, Aamir taught history to the young kids, and Ben, well, he ran a poker night on weekends. Of course, his luck as a gambler seemed to have mysteriously improved after Dexter was hired to be a poker dealer.

"What was my father like?" Adam asked.

She let out a gentle laugh.

"I would have thought you would have known."

"We moved away from him when I was six, I don't remember much before that and the few times I saw him, my mother would always speak badly of him."

"Ah, relationships are tough. What was your father like? Well, I guess that depends on who you ask. I only knew him a short while, Adam, and people tend to hide who they are behind what they do for a living, what they want people to know, and well… I might not have known what made your father tick, but I will tell you this, the last thing on his mind before he died was you."

Adam nodded and opened his hand. Inside was the crumpled piece of paper that still had Zeke's blood on it. "I wish I'd got to know him."

She nodded gently and ran a hand around the back of his head. Upon arriving in Cape Canaveral, she had been adamant they check the address. Some might have said Zeke was self-absorbed, and they wouldn't have been wrong, however, behind the glitz and glamor, the money and the fame, there was a man who had regrets. They all did. A performer, a thief, a businessman, a cabbie and an escort; each of them dealt with life in their own way and formed assumptions about each other but through a rare and unexpected event, they came to realize they were much more than strangers.

"He was a hero!" a familiar voice bellowed from behind them. They turned to see Dexter strolling towards them. There was a limp to each step he took. He grinned and came over and ruffled Adam's hair. "Did I tell you about the time he caught me before I fell down the elevator shaft? Or the time he pulled me out of a crevice? Or the night he took a bullet for me?"

Adam's eyes widened and his chest puffed out a little.

"Yep, your old man was one hell of a guy."

Felicity smiled knowing everything coming out of his mouth was a damn lie. Of course, he had his moments, but she knew the truth.

"Oh, which reminds me," Dexter fished into his pocket and pulled out a flashy gold watch. He bent over slightly and handed it to him. "Your old man would have wanted you to have it."

His eyebrows shot up. "It belonged to him?"

"Sure did."

Adam stared at it with wild-eyed wonder as he took it.

"Thanks, Dexter."

"Go on, on your way, I think your mom was asking about you."

He smiled and thanked them both before slowly walking away.

They watched him, staring at the gold watch until he was out of earshot. Dexter turned and looked out of the observation station, his hands clasped behind him, his chest out and a cheeky grin on his face.

Felicity smiled. “That was a nice thing to say.”

“Ah you know me, I aim to please.”

She chuckled. He put an arm around her and led her away. “So about that date.”

“Dexter.”

“Okay, okay, you can’t blame a guy for trying. But believe me, one of these days you will say yes.”

There was a long pause.

“How about tomorrow?”

“Dexter.”

“Okay, okay.”

“Ask me next week,” she said, nudging him in the ribs. “By the way, was that really his watch?” she asked.

“Of course it was. Would I lie?”

Her brow knit together and she narrowed her eyes. “He didn’t give it to you, did he?”

Dexter cast a sideways glance, and cleared his throat, then winked. "Not exactly."

* * *

THANK YOU FOR READING

If you enjoyed that try out All That Remains or Days of Panic or Rules of Survival. Please take a second to leave a review, even if it's only 10 words. It's much appreciated.

A Plea

Thank you for reading Final Impact. If you enjoyed the book, I would really appreciate it if you would consider leaving a review. Without reviews, an author's books are virtually invisible on the retail sites. It also lets me know what you liked. You can leave a review by visiting the book's page. I would greatly appreciate it. It only takes a couple of seconds.

Thank you — **Jack Hunt**

Newsletter

Thank you for buying Final Impact published by Direct Response Publishing.

Click here to receive special offers, bonus content, and news about new Jack Hunt's books. Sign up for the newsletter. http://www.jackhuntbooks.com/signup/

About the Author

Jack Hunt is the author of horror, sci-fi and post-apocalyptic novels. He currently has over thirty books out. All that Remains series, Cyber Apocalypse series, War Buds Series, three in the Camp Zero series, five books out in the Renegades series, three books in the Agora Virus series, one out in the Armada series, a time travel book called Killing Time, Blackout and another called Mavericks: Hunters Moon. Jack lives on the East coast of North America.

Made in United States
North Haven, CT
23 June 2022

20503045R00236